For Sue ~

LILLIAN'S LEGACY

By Carmen Peone

So glad we've
become friends!,
XOXO

Carmen Peone

ISBN: 978-1-7323356-4-6

This book is a work of fiction deeply rooted in years of research, both oral and written historical fact, and family lore. I pray to have captured the spirit of truth, if not always the precision of fact, and that liberties I have taken will be forgiven.

Cover design and formatting design by Rossano Designs
Published by Painted Hill Press

DEDICATION

To all the girls who aspire to greatness.

CHAPTER 1

August 4, 1875
Northeast Washington Territory

Lillian had never been a deceiver. Until today. She hadn't meant to. Hadn't meant to be so selfish. But when the offer came, it was too good. Would the cost be too high?

That morning, Lillian sat on the edge of the bed and ran a finger over her sister's quilt made from various fabric scraps. Mama said it looked like pairs of weddin' rings looped over the coverlet. She grunted, wondering if she'd ever find a beau to marry. *If so, will Mama stitch me one this fancy?*

"Hannah?" From outside, Lillian's mother, Elizabeth Gardner, called for her sister, the bride.

Lillian stiffened at her mother's voice, knowing she should not be snooping around her sister's belongings. The ceremony would begin soon. Everyone was waiting for the preacher to arrive from Pinckney City near Fort Colville.

She caressed the multi-colored interlinking circles one last time before tucking the quilt back in her sister's parfleche bag. Running a finger over the stiff leather, she wondered what her future wedding might look like.

"Lillian, I need your help!" Her mother's voice bounced through the log cabin, causing Lillian to jerk.

"Coming." Lillian's belly churned like cream agitating into butter. She weaved through Sinyekst guests, who lived in the village northwest of them, admiring their buckskin garments adorned with beads and eagle feathers, and found her mother.

Elizabeth handed her an apple pie and frowned, glancing at her daughter. "What happened to your gown?" She fingered a yellow ribbon in her hair that matched her silky dress as though making sure it wasn't about to fall out.

Lillian smoothed a few wrinkles from her green and pink floral gown, her fingers landing on a dark smear. "I—I'm not—"

"For heaven's sake, child, go clean up."

Child? Lillian trudged to a table lined with desserts and set the pie down. She should not have visited Asa that morning. Shoving through the sea of guests, she found her way to the creek, grabbed a handful of pebbles and scrubbed the dirt from her dress. She hated the bustle. It was useless where they lived. She regretted the day she'd talked her mother into going to Fort Colville where she'd caught the fashion plague. It must have brought her back to her Eastern raising.

Once finished, Lillian gathered the weighted skirt and hustled back to help. "Is this better?" She held out her skirt to her mother, a faint stain still showing.

Elizabeth quit humming and shrugged, a small smile on her face. "I suppose it'll do." She brushed at the stain. "Now, stand tall, honey. You're a woman now. I know it's your birthday, but please, dear, no sulking—"

"What do you want me to do with these, Lizzy?" Phillip Gardner appeared with a basket of bread and cheese in one hand, his walking stick in another.

Sulking? Really! Lillian bit her tongue until she tasted a metallic liquid.

"Where is the new walking stick I had made for you?" Elizabeth's gaze fell to the weathered gray wood. "I like this one better. It fits my hand—"

"Oh, bother." Elizabeth rolled her eyes. She took the basket from her husband and handed it to Lillian. "Why don't you take this around and see if anyone needs a little something to fill their stomachs." She glanced around. "Where is that preacher?"

"Why don't you go sit a spell?" Phillip placed a hand on the small of his wife's back. "He'll be here when he gets here, Lizzy." He nodded to Lillian. "Our daughter will take care of our guests."

"There's no time to rest. Good heavens!" Elizabeth waved at a woman and hurried off in her direction.

"I've never seen her this rattled." Lillian shook her head. "But I will take care of our guests, Pa." She caught a glimpse of the stunning bride, four silk bows trickling down the front of her silk and lace gown. A five-tiered bustle cascaded from behind, melting into a ruffle hemming the skirt. Bows and lace adorned each cuff, and lace enclosed the base of Hannah's neck. Lillian sighed, praying one day she might look as striking as her sister. But doubted it. Her shoulders slumped. She dreamed of wearing the lace veil shading her sister's mahogany dark-brown hair.

Flaming red hair with rogue curls and a bridge of freckles across dainty noses hardly seemed to attract male suitors. At least not in her case. She should not have peeked in her mother's looking glass that morning. The image had imprinted in her mind and she couldn't seem to shake it loose.

Phillip snuck a piece of bread and cheese and gestured toward Lillian. "I trust you will. Now, you better get on and see to their needs before your mama loses her good senses." He motioned to the crowd.

Lillian went from person to person, offering a morsel of food and a fake smile. Women's eyes roamed the length of her dress. Young girls whispered, pointed, and giggled, their hands covering their mouths. Inside, her tummy twisted and her heart ached. *Sulking*, she couldn't shove the word out of her mind. Her cheeks heated. She took a sip of water, quenching the prickled desert in her mouth.

When the basket emptied, she laid it on a make-shift table of two ladders and a board and headed for the barn. Once inside, she inhaled, soaking in the sweet aroma of hay and horse. Asa whinnied, his nose bobbing from across the stall plank boards. She scratched his brown nose, fingered his black mane. "You understand me, don't ya, boy?"

"Who is this?" A woman said from the shadows, her voice thick with a foreign accent.

Lillian flung around, her heart pounding.

The oddly-dressed woman stepped into view. Her hair covered with a white cap tied at her chin and tall, black hat over it, she smiled. She shuffled her frail frame beside Lillian and reached a knotted hand up for Asa to sniff. Lillian stared at her sea-green eyes, a warmth radiating from them.

"What is this beast's name?"

Pulling the words out of her mouth, Lillian said, "Asa. His name's Asa."

"He is a beauty, *le*, yes?"

Lillian relaxed. "He is." She continued to study the elder woman's attire: a yellow and green printed kerchief tied around her neck, a red flannel cloak wrapped around her shoulders, an apron over a flannel skirt, and black shoes with metal buckles, her flannel petticoat peeking from underneath the hem of her skirt.

"You think I dress oddly, do you not?"

Lillian's cheeks heated. "Pardon me. I have never seen a woman such as you before."

The woman laughed. "That is all right. Many have not."

"Where do you come from?"

"A place called Myddfai in southeast Wales where grass is green all year round, covering plenty of rolling hills dotted with sheep and cattle and horses. Have you heard of it?"

"I have not. Is it far? Is that why you dress the way you do?"

"*Le*, yes, and *le*," the woman said with a bright grin. She watched Lillian, her eyes appearing curious. "I am on my way north and am hoping to stop for a rest. Both my mount and I could use fresh water and shade. It is nice to see friendly faces. And what do they call you?"

"Lillian."

"What a lovely name."

"And you? What is your name?"

"*Braf i gwrdd a chi*, nice to meet you. I am Doctor S.M. Maddox. But my mother called me Mali." Doctor Maddox winked at Lillian and stroked Asa's neck. "It looks to be a celebration today, *le*? I hope I am not intruding."

Lillian nodded. She felt the joy of meeting a strange yet alluring woman drain from her. "My sister is getting married today."

5

"A happy day, then." Doctor Maddox leaned an arm against the top rail. "But you do not look pleased."

"Oh, but I am."

"Oh…?"

"It's my birthday today, but no one seems to notice." *Sulking.* Perhaps her mother was right. Heat flashed in her cheeks. *I need to learn to keep my mouth closed. Keep my feelings to myself.*

"And how old are you?"

"Sixteen."

"A woman, then."

Lillian lengthened her spine. "I suppose so."

Doctor Maddox smiled and patted Lillian's shoulder.

"Would you like to join us?" She hoped the woman might be a grand distraction for her and her mother.

"I would be delighted." Doctor Maddox followed Lillian into the late morning sun, her arm looped around her new friend's.

"And who is this?" Elizabeth held a hand out to the woman with the black hat seeming to reach for the clouds.

Lillian stepped aside. "Her name is Mali, I mean Doctor Maddox, and she's from Wales."

"Oh? Where in Wales?" Elizabeth arched a brow.

The doctor filled her in and then asked, "So your daughter is getting married today? You must be beside yourself."

"I am." Elizabeth took the woman's arm and led her to a table loaded with food. "What brings you this far north?"

"Where's Mama?" Hannah said as she rushed to her sister's side. "If the preacher doesn't come soon, I'm afraid Leslie will either faint in his roasting suit or marry us himself."

Lillian sighed. "Over there."

Hannah tipped her head. "Who is she with?"

"Doctor Mali Maddox," Lillian said. "She's from Wales."

"A woman doctor? Marvelous!" Hannah's gaze sized up her sister. "I suppose you will remain a homemaker, if and when you find a suitable man."

"If?" Lillian's heart sank.

"You know what I mean. You may choose to remain here and care for our folks when they are old and too feeble to care for the ranch is all I meant. And be like, you know, Mama." She giggled. "Don't be so sensitive, Lilly."

"Sensitive?" Would she ever be as bold and daring as her horse-racing sister had been at her age?

"Oh, and happy birthday, little sister." Hannah glanced around. "I need to find Pa. Have you seen him? He will know what to do." She gathered her gown and scurried to her father's side.

Lillian shrank. She dragged herself into the cabin and poured herself a cup of water. On a shelf above a worktable were herbs her mother stored in glass jars. She searched for the right one to calm her nerves. "There you are." She took a jar of dried hawthorn leaves, made tea, and sat in the quiet cabin.

Moments later, the door slammed open. "What are you doing in here?" Delbert had never looked so handsome in his black jacket, tan trousers, and black Stetson set low on his head.

"Taking a break."

7

"Ma's lookin' for ya," Delbert said. "Best hurry before she melts." He turned to leave then stopped. "By the way, happy birthday, kid. Now quit sulkin' and get to work."

How many times would she have to hear that word today?

"He's here!" Elizabeth's voice rang throughout the cabin.

Lillian closed her eyes for a moment, inhaled a big breath, and let it out between her clenched teeth. "This day cannot end soon enough." She took a seat in the back row, by Doctor Maddox, who glanced at her and grinned. Lillian smiled back. The glint of Leslie's sword caught her attention. He looked dapper in his army coat, cap, and trousers. Shiny buttons dotted down his uniform jacket, standing military straight, his gaze on his bride. His high collar didn't seem to distract him in the heat.

"Now that you are a woman, perhaps you would like to join me and learn additional healing ways." Doctor Maddox patted Lillian's hand, bringing her out of her pity. "I have had a marvelous conversation with your mother. She says you have a way with herbs."

"Oh, I could never leave." *But why not?* Here was her chance to prove she could be someone. Someone other than "a suitable wife and mother." Her chest clenched. Why wouldn't she cling to such an offer? Would there be another one in her lifetime? She wrung her hands.

"Think about it. I will leave after the evening meal."

As the preacher spoke about love, reciting Bible verses, Lillian could not help but wonder if her mother wanted her out of the home. Hannah was always her favorite. Their mother had traveled countless times to the Sinyekst village across the river to watch her race horses. Stitched her the prettiest dresses. Made sure her birthday was special. *I get the scraps.* Garments. Shoes. Books. Toys. Could she muster the courage to leave? Her tummy twirled. Perhaps by staying she could prove her value. Then again, leaving may be the only way.

CHAPTER 2

Lillian stabbed a chunk of venison, swirled it in brown gravy, and plopped it in her mouth. The doctor's invitation haunted her. She chewed and pondered. *What would it be like to be on my own? Learning. Exploring. It took Mama courage to travel west as a mail-order bride.* Could she be so brave?

"Wasn't the ceremony lovely?" Hannah plopped on a bench beside Lillian and looped an arm around one of her sister's and pulled her close. "This is the best day of my life! My dress, the ceremony—everything—it's perfect!" She took a sip from Lillian's tin cup. "Do you like my ring?" She shoved it in Lillian's face, and then at Doctor Maddox.

"It's pretty." With each pretentious word, the doc's offer seemed more and more inviting. It was time Lillian made a life of her own. Followed her dreams. Saw the world. She'd been stuffed in her corner of the territory for long enough. She could learn new skills. Help people.

"I can't wait to leave tonight. Start my life with my soldier!"

I can't wait either! Lillian grinned. "It will be a grand adventure." She held back from asking if she was sure she

11

could settle down and be the wife of a soldier after tearing up the trails racing horseback for the last several years. She laughed inside, thinking of how Leslie would have his hands full with a spitfire like Hannah. A giggle escaped her lips. Her sister tipped her head, brows pinched.

"Your ring is charming," Doctor Maddox said. "And where will you live?"

"Fort Walla Walla. Leslie," Hannah cleared her throat, "Lieutenant Archer, belongs with the "E" Company." She spoke as though he was a captain.

"Where are you headed?" Lillian said to Doctor Maddox.

"To the Kettle Falls area. Doctor Finlay used to treat folks in those parts and now that he's gone, they are in need of medical attention." She chuckled. "They think I am a man."

Lillian caught Hannah's grin. "Why is that?"

"Well, even though I have a medical license," Doctor Maddox said, "woman doctors are frowned upon. Even today. So I used my deceased husband's first initial "S" and my first name "M." I am sure they have not yet learned he's passed on and think I am he." She took a sip of her tea. "This is delicious. You must tell me, *merch*, girl, what herbs you used to make it."

"I would love to." Lillian felt her heart flutter.

"If you want to know about herbs, talk with my mother," Hannah said. "She is the expert."

Lillian's heart sank like a rock in a river. She bit the inside of her cheek to keep from starting a squabble.

Doctor Maddox took a bite of cake as a hint of pink crept across her face. Under the table, she patted Lillian's knee as though understanding her embarrassment.

Lillian finished her cake while well-wishers congratulated her sister on her marriage. Some had the nerve to mention they hoped Lillian would someday find a suitable fellow, as though she was the ugliest girl in the territory. When she could take no more, she fled to the barn—her safe haven.

She opened Asa's gate and slid inside, not caring if her dress became soiled. She wrapped her arms around his neck and sobbed. After a long moment, she said to her horse, "Can I ever be someone special? Can I leave here? Leave Papa? I feel he needs me. The stump of his leg only troubles him as he ages. Tell me what to do."

Asa nudged her.

"You all right?"

Lillian's body tensed at the sound of her father's voice. She wiped her eyes. "I am. Just wanted to check on Asa. Get away from the crowd."

"You always were a loner," he said, his voice soothing.

She shrugged. "I like the quiet."

"It's not a bad thing."

Phillip opened the gate and limped to his daughter. He drew her into a firm hug. "Happy Birthday, Lilly Pad. I'm sorry your sister had to have her wedding on your birthday. It really was the only day. Leslie has to get ready to head to Walla Walla and settle him and your sister in before the snow flies."

Lillian held onto her father. "I know. It's okay, Papa."

"I'm going to go help your mother. Why don't you clean up a bit and join me?"

Lillian nodded. She watched him limp away. No, she could not leave him. She would continue to work alongside her mother and help doctor those moving into the area, along with the Sinyekst, and learn traditional medicinal ways from their healer.

She took a moment to brush Asa, wiped as much of his hair from her clothing and body as she could, and went in search of her father.

Just as she stepped from the barn, Doctor Maddox caught her arm.

"Have you decided yet?" The square-jawed woman stepped into the barn. "I am in need of a good nurse."

"But I have no education."

"I will teach you, my dear."

Lillian watched her Pa fill a woman's glass from the wooden pitcher he'd carved for one of her mother's birthdays, wince as he rubbed his leg, and limp toward the next person. "I must remain here and help my father."

Doctor Maddox nodded. "I understand. But if you change your mind, I won't be far. Me and my old nag, Chwim, we travel the pace of turtle." She patted Lillian's shoulder. "I wish you much happiness on your birthday."

"Thank you. And I am thankful for the offer."

The doctor fished in her satchel and pulled out an elongated pouch. "This is for you." She handed it to Lillian and hobbled away.

Lillian went to the other side of the barn and opened the pouch. She slid out an apparatus and tipped her head. "What in heaven's name…?" She examined the long, wooden hollow tube with a bell-shape on one end and a more flat, circular piece on the other. *What could this be?* It kind of looked like one of those eyepieces their neighbor Jack Dalley had. She tried to look through it. Blew in it and decided only Doctor Maddox would have the answer.

She scurried to the barn, through the crowds, and into the cabin. Where had she gone? She found her mother. "Have you seen Doctor Maddox?"

"I have not." Elizabeth reached for Lillian, but she whisked away.

Lillian walked around, searching for the aged healer. When the sun was almost down, she gave up and went to the Columbia River, which snaked just west of the cabin, and found a sandy spot to think of all the reasons she should stay put.

All she could think about was the one reason she should go: to become someone special. Someone who could manage herself. Alone. Maybe then her mother would love her as much as she loved Hannah.

CHAPTER 3

Lillian waved to her sister and new brother-in-law. She went to her room and changed into a work dress. Part of her was happy Hannah was gone—she would no longer be under her sister's wayward shadow—and part of her was sad. Hannah's leaving left a void in her heart. Fort Walla Walla seemed so far away. Loving her sister was not the issue. She simply wanted to feel as important.

Outside, the Gardners bid farewell to the last of the guests. Phillip and Elizabeth sank into the rockers they'd pulled outside for a few elders. After a few moments of peace, Phillip took hold of his wife's hand, pressing a tender kiss to her skin.

"Suppose we need to clean up, huh?" Phillip rose and snatched the wooden pitcher off a table.

Elizabeth dabbed her eyes with a floral embroidered handkerchief. "Suppose you're right."

"I'll go feed the horses and check on the livestock," Delbert said as he scurried toward the barn.

"Lillian, dear," Elizabeth said, "won't you help me clear these tables? Maybe you can start heating water for dishes."

"Yes, Mama." Lillian ground her teeth, her thoughts stuck on the way her sister flaunted herself and her ring to anyone who would look and listen. *I'll never act so brash.* She plucked a washtub from a nail on the side of the log cabin, dropped it beside the fire pit, found a bucket, and filled it with water. Time and again, she filled the bucket, stomped to the washtub and poured.

"What are you doing?" Elizabeth shoved her hands on her hips. "Heat the water then fill the tub." She studied her daughter. "What has gotten into you? This was your sister's big day. You should be happy for her."

"I am," Hannah said through gritted teeth. Her chest tight, she started a fire and hooked a kettle of water to a metal tripod. She chastised herself for reacting to her mother in such a disrespectful way, but after all, it wasn't just her sister's wedding. It was also her birthday.

She bit her lip, holding in tears. The last thing she wanted was pity. Knew her attitude was selfish and absurd. Then why did she feel so insignificant? *Lord, fill me with gratitude.*

When everyone seemed busy, she snuck into her room and packed. She shoved extra clothing, jerked venison and salmon, dried fruit, pinches of herbs into pouches for tea and healing, and the wooden thing Mali had given her. She plopped down on her bed, wondering how she would sneak her over-stuffed parfleche to the barn.

Then she remembered the pouch Spupaleena, Hannah's adopted Sinyekst aunt from across the river, had given her when she was a little girl. She dug it out from the bottom of her bureau and held it up. "Perfect." She took the food and wooden thingamajig out of her parfleche and tucked it into the pouch. The strap was long enough she could sling it over her shoulder.

18

But for now, she hid her bags under a quilt.

With a smile and a light step, she went to the fire and finished washing dishes. No one seemed to notice her absence. She felt completely invisible. Catching up with Mali, Doctor Maddox, was the solution she didn't know she needed. Until now.

A giggle came from inside the barn, so Lillian went to investigate. Delbert and a pretty blonde were chatting and giggling, a bit too close for comfort. Lillian's ears warmed. Hadn't everyone gone home? Then again, one diversion was out of the way. All she needed was a distraction for her folks.

She was placing the dishes back in the cupboard when an idea struck her. She shoved plates and cups in their normal places on the shelf and went in search of her father. He was helping a man hook his horse up to a wagon. *Must be the blonde's Pa.*

"Pa." Lillian noticed weariness etched on his face.

"Hello, Lilly Pad. Get the dishes done?" Fatigue seemed to slur his words.

Should I leave him when he's this tired? Who would help take care of him with both daughters gone? Another giggle wafted from the barn. *Delbert will be around.* "When you're finished here, why don't you take Mama on a stroll up on the hill and watch the sunset. You know the place. I'll saddle your horses for you, or Delbert and I can hitch the buckboard—"

"I don't know." Phillip held up a hand. "I think your ma's pretty worn out."

"What better way to end a wonderful day, your daughter's wedding, with just the two of you, watching the beautiful summer color fade in Mama's favorite place? I'll make you some tea for your leg."

"Oh, I don't know…"

The man thanked Phillip for helping him fix a broken loin strap on the horse harness and encouraged him to take his daughter's advice, winking at Lillian.

Lillian held her hands behind her back so she wouldn't seem desperate, praying he'd agree to her suggestion.

"All right. I'll see if she wants to go."

"No, Papa, I'll saddle the horses and fetch a quilt. Don't give her a reason to decline." Lillian gathered her skirt and rushed into the cabin before her father could give her any more excuses.

Elizabeth sat in her rocker, Bible clutched to her chest, her eyes closed. Her feet pushed and rested, pushed and rested, as the chair gently rocked. Lillian found the kettle. How would she get her mother up and moving? *Herbs!*

Lillian picked out a jar of peppermint, found the herbs to ease her father's pain, grabbed the kettle, and went outside to brew two cups of strong tea. She chuckled as she poured boiling water into the cups, feeling somewhat sinister, but convincing herself it was for a good reason. She would leave a girl and come back a woman of value. Or so she hoped. It wouldn't be long, perhaps several months, she told herself.

After all, it looked as though her birthday would be forgotten. Once again overshadowed by the infamous Hannah Gardner, woman horse racer.

Lillian went inside. "Here, Mama, drink this."

Elizabeth opened her eyes and took the cup. "Mmm, peppermint. My favorite. Thank you, dear." She inhaled the steam circling her nose and took a sip. "Where is your father?"

"He has a surprise for you." Lillian smiled. "But first, drink your tea."

"Oh? What is it?"

"A surprise, remember?" Lillian spun around and went back outside. Goosebumps formed on her arms. *This will be a grand adventure!* She then took her father's tea to him, imagining how delighted Mali will be when she saw her. The man and his family had just pulled out, and the blonde Delbert had been absorbed with was in the wagon bed, her lips pulled into a pout. Phillip and her brother stood side by side, watching and waving as their wagon rattled down the rutted path. A light breeze caught the dust as it swirled behind them.

"Here's your tea, Pa." Lillian turned to Delbert. "Will you help me in the barn?"

"Nope. I'm goin' fishin'."

Fishing! The word sang in her ears.

Delbert spun on his heels and headed for the barn.

Lillian walked fast to keep up with his long strides. "I'm planning a quiet evening for Pa and Mama in the hills so they can watch the sun set together. Will you help me saddle their horses?"

Delbert snorted. "Why would you do that?"

"They—it's been a hectic day. They deserve time to settle before going to bed."

"No."

"Why?"

"Like I said, I'm goin' fishin'." Delbert pushed her aside and took his rod from the wall. "They're tired, leave them be." He pushed past her and headed for the river.

"Why you…!"

Buttercup, Elizabeth's palomino mare, whinnied. Lillian kicked the dirt and got two halters and a brush. She quickly groomed both the mare and Sammy, her father's aged gelding, and saddled them. When done, she led them outside, slid on their bridles, and tied them to the hitching rail.

Her parents met her on the cabin porch, her mother's brows pinched.

Elizabeth took Phillip's hand in hers. "Thank you for the lovely gesture, dear, but we are simply too exhausted to travel—"

"Travel? Your favorite spot is just up the hill. It's a short ride." Her voice hitched. *Do I sound frantic?* "You won't be long. I'll have the rest of the house tidy when you come back.

"Let's go, Lizzy," Phillip said. "We don't have to stay long."

Long enough for me to leave is all. "He's right. The sun will set soon. You won't be gone long." Lillian took hold of her mother's hand and led her to the mare.

"All right. A short ride might do us good." Elizabeth kissed Buttercup's nose and stepped on.

Lillian waved them off and rushed to the cabin.

She tidied up a few things, slung the pack over her shoulder, grabbed one of Phillip's deer skinning knives, her parfleche, and headed out the door. When almost to the barn, she remembered a blanket. And her brown Stetson. She dropped her parfleche and dashed back to the cabin. She chose one of her father's Hudson's Bay trade blankets and bounced down the porch stair. After taking a couple of steps she came to a halt, her cowboy hat tipping to the side. Delbert stood by her bag, hands on his hips. She settled her hat on her head, lifted her chin, and strode toward him, her knees quivering.

"Going somewhere?"

Lillian bit her bottom lip.

"You sounded too eager for everyone to leave. And now I see why. Where ya headed?" Delbert tapped her bag with the tip of his fishing pole.

"I—I"—she held out her pouch—"I am bringing Doctor Maddox some supplies."

"Why?" Delbert took a couple of steps closer and reached for the parfleche.

Lillian shoved him away and grabbed the stiff bag. "While we were in the barn talking, she mentioned she had a long way to travel. Mama and I fixed her some goodies and I'm taking them to her. She's just up the river a ways." She stood taller. "Mama knows I'm going."

"Does she?"

"Yes." Lillian lifted her chin, grabbed the parfleche, and marched to the barn.

"I guess we'll find out when they get back."

Lillian grabbed a horse brush.

"Yes, we will!"

She rushed around and brushed, saddled, bridled, and jumped on Asa, speeding out of the barn and on her way.

On her way to freedom!

CHAPTER 4

It was almost dark when Lillian found the doctor's camp. A small fire danced across the rocks surrounding it. "Doctor Maddox?" She slid off her horse and strode closer. A figure leaned against a tall ponderosa pine. "Mali?" She tied Asa to a tree limb and crept over to the woman. Was it too late? Had the woman died before they could work together? Before she could learn her form of medicine?

She placed a hand on the woman's warm shoulder and gently shook her. "Doctor Maddox?" The woman jumped and screamed, sending Lillian tumbling backward.

"*Oh, my,* pardon my fright!" Doctor Maddox crawled to Lillian's side. "Are you all right?" She examined the girl, brushing dirt and debris from her arms and dress.

Lillian laughed. "Yes, I am. I thought you were dead!"

"*Ma flin da fi,* sorry to have startled you. I was merely resting my eyes." The doctor smiled. "Have you changed your mind?"

Lillian rose to her knees, nodding. "I have. I want to learn your ways of medicine. To help people in need. Learn what the contraption you gave me is. Speaking

25

of…!" She stopped to catch her breath and fetch the wooden instrument, holding it out to the doctor. "What is this?"

Doctor Maddox took it from her and caressed the wooden tube. "This was my husband's stethoscope." For a moment she held the monaural device to her heart. "It's made of the finest cherry wood one can find."

"Why would you give it to me?"

Doctor Maddox smiled. "Because I knew you needed to check your own heart. It seems to beat with young, vigorous life, but there is something holding you back. I can see it in your eyes. Hear it in your voice. A missing spark of youth."

Lillian dropped her chin. "I suppose so."

"Did you tell your folks you were joining me?"

"They will know soon enough." Lillian hugged herself. "Like you said, I'm a woman now. Can I not make my own decisions?"

"And how would you feel if they left and did not inform you?" Doctor Maddox rose.

Lillian shrugged. "My brother knows." She pushed to her feet, brushed dirt from her hands.

"Mm. It is a good thing I have already spoken with them," Doctor Maddox said. "In the future, I expect you to be frank with me. I will not tolerate any degree of conniving." Her expression softened. "Now, I am tired and need to rest. It will be a long day's travel tomorrow."

"Yes, ma'am," Lillian said, feeling foolish for her devious behavior.

The doctor spread out her bedroll. "You better take care of your horse and get some sleep. We will have a long day tomorrow."

Lillian unsaddled Asa, led him to the river for a drink, and tied him to the trunk of a tree near a patch of grass. What kind of proof would she need? She spread her blanket on the ground, using the horse blanket as a pillow, and laid down. Twinkling stars shone brightly. Her mind raced with wonder. Who would be their first patient? What kind of adventure was before them? Then fear pricked at her. Would they come across thugs or bandits as her father had? Would any of them try to harm them? For what seemed like hours, her mind fiddled with various scenarios. Then finally her eyelids grew heavy.

August 5

Lillian woke to crunching footsteps. Through blurry, sleep-filled eyes, hooves came closer then stopped. She shot to one elbow, pulling a knife from her boot.

"Put that thing away." A man said. She recognized her brother's voice.

"What are you doing here?" Lillian put a finger to her mouth and glanced at Doctor Maddox's empty bedroll. *Where was she?* She scanned the area and saw nothing, wondering if she'd gone to clean up at the river.

"Why didn't you come back last night?"

"I'm not coming back."

Delbert dismounted and grabbed his sister's arm. "Ma and Pa are worried sick."

"What for? No one even considered my birthday. As usual, everything was about Hannah."

"It was her wedding day."

"She could have picked any day!"

Delbert let go of her and sighed. "Suppose your right."

Lillian rubbed her arm, her lips pinched. Had her brother for once agreed with her?

"What do you plan to do?"

Lillian lifted her chin. "Doctor Maddox has asked me to join her and learn her doctoring ways. I've accepted. I'm a woman. I can make my own decisions."

"Woo-wee! A woman. Let me get a good look at ya." He stepped backward and frowned. "If you're a woman, you should have had the nerve to speak to our folks about it and not sneak off into the night like a yellow-bellied greenhorn."

"Well, now, I suppose you're right. But…" Lillian shrugged. "I knew they'd disagree." Her brother's face flashed a different regard, as though he knew something and had decided to keep it to himself. She wondered if she should ask. Or was this his way of jesting with her?

"How will you know if you don't ask?" Delbert said. "Besides. If you would have stuck around, you would have made it to your party."

Lillian's face warmed. "A party for me?"

"Yeah. That's why they didn't want to go watch the sun drop."

"Oh?"

"But you just kept pushing." Delbert shook his head, seeming to enjoy her squirm from her own humiliation. "Why do you think I came back?"

"Why?" Lillian put a hand to her neck.

"To help them get ready for the party so they could go and enjoy the sunset. Which they didn't. They started out then came back. They were more interested in your birthday than a darned-ole painted sky."

"If that were true, they would have told Hannah to have her wedding on another day."

"Maybe."

28

CARMEN PEONE

Doctor Maddox appeared from the direction of the Columbia River. "Well, *helo,* hello, Delbert. *Shwd mae,* how are you?"

"Fine, ma'am—I mean Doc—Doctor Maddox, ma'am." Delbert's face shaded red as an apple. With a thumb and forefinger, he tipped the front of his hat.

"We need to be on our way." Doctor Maddox nodded to Delbert. "I wish you and your family well." She shuffled to her bedroll and began packing.

"So, that's your answer. You're leaving to practice medicine."

Lillian wrung her hands. "Yes, I am. Please tell Ma and Pa I love them and I'll write."

"You'll write. That's it?"

Lillian's face heated, her body quivering. "I have to pack." She gave Delbert a quick hug.

"Hold on." Delbert pulled a cloth-wrapped package from one of his saddlebags. "This is from Ma. You'll get the rest of your gifts when you decide to become a real woman and come home." He mounted, whirled his horse around, and galloped off.

Fighting tears, Lillian tugged the twine that held the cloth around the package. She unwound the cord, stuck it in her skirt pocket, and unwrapped the cloth that revealed a leather-bound book, an ink well, and a long wooden box. The journal cover read "Lillian's Legacy." She pursed her lips, allowing a few tears to roll down her cheeks. She wiped her eyes and thumbed through the blank pages.

She sank to her knees, set the book and ink well on her lap, and turned the box over in her hands. Inside was a fountain pen and eyedropper. She gasped, admiring the gold nib. Not only would she learn medicine, she would

29

also be able to record her travels, sights, sounds, experiences. A chill snaked up her back.

She was about to embark on the journey of a lifetime. With a real female medical doctor. She pressed the book against her chest. *Be happy for me, Mama.*

"About ready?" Doctor Maddox motioned to the gifts. "For your birthday?"

"Yes, ma'am." Lillian tucked the book and pen set in her buckskin pouch and rolled up her bedding. She wanted to go back and thank her mother. Hug her before heading out. But she feared she would not have the nerve to follow the doctor if she went home. Maybe she would follow her for a few weeks and then come back. Would that be enough time to learn?

She watered and packed her horse, stuffed a piece of jerked venison in her mouth, and mounted Asa. Excitement, fear, regret, it all swirled in her gut and caught in her throat. Her spine straight and hands held firmly to the rein, she urged her gelding forward.

CHAPTER 5

Lillian inhaled. A balmy afternoon breeze swirling off the river caressed her face. "Where will we go first?"

"Our first stop will be where Hudson's Bay Fort Colvile used to be," Doctor Maddox said. "And to Meyers Falls. There are people who need medical attention in the community. Then we will visit the military Fort Colville near Pinckney City. There is a surgeon at the hospital who can help stock my supplies. You can make your first post to your folks there."

Lillian nodded, wondering if the woman realized how long it would take for the note to reach her mother. As they rode, her mind slid to Hannah, her sister's headstrong ways, and her past horse racing shenanigans. She chuckled, knowing Officer Leslie Archer had his hands full. "E" company's duties would seem simple compared to handling her sister.

She tried to relax into Asa's fluid sway, dreaming about helping women and children, saving lives, and learning Doctor Maddox's methods and intertwining them with what her mother had taught her about the healing powers of medicinal plants. Hopefully when they stopped to rest or for a quick meal, she would show the doctor her pouches of herbs.

You should have told them. Coward.

Delbert's words needled her. To push them out of her head, she thought about what her first journal entry would be. Mali's invitation. The beauty of the territory. Its smells and colors. Asa pranced, startling her out of her muses.

She reached over to pat her gelding's neck when a squeal gushed from his throat. He darted to the right. From somewhere a woman screamed. Or was it her? She tried to rein her horse around and get control. But he kept side-running. They slammed into a tree. Lillian groaned, pain pulsating from her leg. The shriek came again. Who was it? "Mali?"

Doctor Maddox circled her horse, her focus behind them. "Hold on, Lillian!"

Asa reared and bucked. "Whoa, boy!" Lillian flew off and landed in the dirt, face down. Asa dashed up the trail several yards, stopped, and turned around, his chest heaving. Lillian struggled to her feet.

Behind them came a woman screaming and running at them, carrying a child, blood splattering them both. Doctor Maddox slid off her horse and dropped the reins. She untied her medical satchel and rushed to meet them.

Lillian didn't know whether to grab her horse or follow the doctor. She decided to follow her companion. "What can I do?" She took one look at the boy's leg, covered her mouth, and turned to vomit. She retched until nothing came out, her head light and fuzzy. There was nothing she could do but sink to the ground before she fell.

Doctor Maddox waved the woman closer. "Come and sit while I take a look at the boy." She dropped her bag on the ground. "You his mother?"

The quivering woman nodded, her face pale. She kept her gaze on her son.

Doctor Maddox opened the metal trap fur traders used to catch small game. "Pull him out." The child screamed, clinging to the frail-looking woman.

The boy's leg slid out of the trap, and Doctor Maddox flung the steel jaw to the side. It snapped shut and hit the ground. "Do you know who owns the trap?" Doctor Maddox frowned, fished two glass bottles and bandages from her bag, and went to work cleaning the wounds. "*Ma flin da fi*, sorry, but I do not have anything to take away his pain. I am in need of more supplies."

"I do," Lillian said.

Doctor Maddox nodded at her. Lillian shot to her feet and rushed to Asa. His head flung up as she approached. She spoke with a soothing tone that seemed to calm him. Her legs shaking, she untied her parfleche and set it on the ground. She sniffed each little pouch until she found the right scent and ran back to the boy.

"Here, chew on this." Lillian handed the boy a piece of bark. The boy whimpered and hid his face in his mother's chest.

She took hold of it and shoved it in her son's mouth. "Do as the woman says." The woman held her boy close, rubbing his back. She closed her red-rimmed eyes.

"What is it?" said Doctor Maddox.

"Willow bark," Lillian said. "Have you heard of it?"

Doctor Maddox nodded. "I use it all the time. Meant to get some but have not had time. Why don't you make some strong tea for him to drink? It'll be easier for him."

She bound the last of the bandages with cloth strips and sat back, addressing the woman, "What is your name?"

"Vera." She closed her eyes and rocked her son.

Doctor Maddox glanced at Lillian and smiled. "That is a lovely name. And what do you call the boy?"

"Charlie."

"Do you know who owns the trap?"

She shook her head, squeezed her eyes.

Lillian wondered if it was the woman's husband and she was protecting him. Perhaps protecting herself. Faded dirt stuck to both Vera and the boy. Charlie's tattered trouser legs came above his ankles. Vera's tan dress was torn at the shoulder, her golden braid a matted mess.

"Why don't you fetch them something cold to drink?" Doctor Maddox gestured to her canteen.

Lillian found a tin cup and the canteen and hurried back, handing the cool water to Vera. She took a sip and offered it to Charlie. He drank, shook the container, and held it out. Lillian filled it up again and fetched a few slices of jerked venison and gave it to Vera.

"Thank you." Vera ripped off a small piece for herself and gave the rest to her son.

"Where have you been?" A rugged-looking man appeared from the trees carrying a martin pelt in one hand and a skinning knife in the other.

Lillian breathed in small breaths. The man stunk like a week-old skunk carcass frying in the desert. She covered her nose with the crook of an arm. His threadbare trousers bore dark-red stains down the legs. Dirt blemished his white linen shirt, turning it various shades of charcoal. Bits of debris clung to his brown beard. She cringed at his dark teeth—what there was left of them.

"Robert!" Vera stiffened, her eyes wide. "Charlie's leg got caught in the trap." She ducked her head.

In three long strides, the man slapped the sniveling child on the top of the head. "Is that right, boy?"

A whimpering Charlie clung to his mom and nodded.

"It was an accident, I swear." Vera's body shook, her gaze cast down. She clung to her son in a protective manner.

Robert grabbed the woman by her hair and pulled her to her feet. Lillian scrambled to hers and shoved the man. He released his grip on Vera and backhanded Lillian, sending her tripping backward. She pressed a hand to her stinging face. He grabbed Vera by the arm and shook her.

"Let her go!" Lillian grabbed his hand and sank her teeth into his flesh until he released Vera.

"Enough!" Doctor Maddox hollered to Lillian.

"He can't treat them like that."

Doctor Maddox took hold of Lillian's arm, gentle but firm. "It is not our concern."

"Not our concern?" Lillian shouted. "The boy cannot care for himself." Spotting a stick on the ground, she rushed to it and beat the man's head and back until he fled.

"I'll be back for them," he hollered, "they're mine!"

"They are not property! They are living souls!" Lillian tossed the stick at him and waited until his back disappeared behind the trees.

"You shouldn't have done that." Vera's eyes watered. "He'll be harder on us, now!" She turned to Doctor Maddox. "Thank you for your kindness. We must be on our way."

"Let me fetch you more provisions." When Vera tried to refuse, Doctor Maddox put up a hand and with Lillian's help fixed her a bag of jerked venison, hardtack, and dried fruit. *Bydded duw gyda chi,* God be with you."

35

Vera held her son's hand as they slinked out of view.

"Why can't we help them?" The words clogged Lillian's throat. "They look like whipped dogs."

"It is our job to assist and let go."

"But they're in danger."

"She was right, you know." Doctor Maddox kneeled to collect her medical supplies. "There are boundaries we must never cross. Ones like today that make the situation worse. Robert will beat her for disobeying him and most likely harm the boy in his blind rage."

Tears stung Lillian's eyes. "But he's a little boy."

"Yes, that is true. But we need wisdom and discernment to know when to step away and when to swing." Doctor Maddox smiled. "I had no idea you were so feisty. I feel somewhat protected with you by my side."

Lillian grunted but relaxed. She helped the doctor gather her belongings. "But you do believe they're in danger?"

"Not concerning death. He needs the woman to cook and…"

"And?"

Doctor Maddox smiled, a twinkle in her eyes. "I was going to say clean. But as you saw, I'm not sure she knows much about that."

Lillian scrunched her nose. "He smelled like a day-old carcass."

"That he did." Doctor Maddox chuckled and placed the last of her tools in her satchel. "You will learn the ways as we go. Have patience and next time, wait for my summons. For your own safety. What if he would have attacked you? Killed you with his knife? I would have had to drag you back to your mother. How would she have handled seeing you dead?"

"Probably not well." Lillian chewed her bottom lip.

"Women like us"—Mali tapped her chest—"healers, it is our duty to leave others with a legacy of hope."

Hope. Lillian nodded, recalling scripture in Jeremiah referring to hope and a future. She understood the need for reassurance.

CHAPTER 6

That evening, Lillian took a stroll along a stream coming from the hills and spilling into the Columbia River. Images of Charlie's bloody leg haunted her. Prayers of protection for him and Vera swirled around her head. She hoped they could someday escape Robert's cruelty.

To keep her sorrow at bay, she explored the area, knowing they were close to where Doctor Finlay had lived. Or so her father had described to her about the time he was beaten by thugs and left for dead.

He spoke about how the kind, aged doctor had taken him in, amputated his mangled leg, and cared for him. She loved hearing the story of when their neighbor and her father's cattle ranch partner Jack Dalley, her mother, and Spupaleena had trekked upriver in spring's harsh weather to find him and bring him home. It was like she could feel Doctor Finlay's spirit with her. She would have liked to meet him. Thank him. Learn from him.

She found a spot on a bed of tan grass and settled herself, journal in hand. She unfolded the fabric and took the fountain pen from its box.

The soft, leather journal smelled as fresh as the day she imagined it was created. She prayed her mama would forgive her. Her father too. Hoped they'd understand why she had to join Doctor Maddox.

She cracked open the pages and fanned them in the warm evening air. Then thumbed to the first page.

Day one and two.

She wished to inscribe the date but had no idea what it was. Perhaps along the way, someone would. She would enter it then.

At the top she penned:

"It is our duty to leave others with a legacy of hope."
Doctor Mali Maddox, 1875

No matter where her journey decided to bring her, Lillian felt those words would be her life's proclamation.

Following Doctor Maddox, an oddly dressed Welsh woman who wears much flannel, a cap, buckled shoes, and a tall black hat, was the wisest decision I have ever made.

I do wish Hannah and Leslie much happiness. But it is time for me to carve out a life of my own. Beginning today, I vow to leave all ill-will behind me. This is an adventure I had not expected, yet find myself clinging to as if it were my last breath.

I thought today would be a lovely ride north from where we had camped for the night. It was far from peaceful. We were not too far from the cabin when Delbert found me. It broke my heart when he told me I was a coward, but was happy he did not drag me home. I think he realized at my age, he too needed time to figure out who he was and to discover God's plan for him in this enormous world.

Today, however, makes me wonder if I am cut out for a life of medicine. We came upon a woman and her young son. Filth covered them. Their clothing nothing but rags held by weak threads. Her husband's odor made me gag. If I hadn't already retched, I would have from the smell permeating from his hide. And what a vile no-account polecat! I know that is no sort of talk for a lady, and mama would tan my hide if she ever heard me speak that way, but it is simply the truth. I have never encountered anyone like him before. It is appalling!

To mistreat his wife and child knowing it was his metal trap that caught poor Charlie's leg. It brought tears to my eyes. The boy and Vera were as frightened as a rabbit being chased by a bobcat.

I did not think, not a lick, when I picked up a stick and beat him until he fled. I have never felt so emboldened before. Even though she reprimanded me for meddling, Doctor Maddox seemed proud, and that was a delightful feeling. One I have not felt for some time.

Shadows never sparkle like the sun.

Lillian rested her pen on the journal and closed her eyes. She let the sound of tumbling water soothe her, praying someday, someway, the good Lord would send her a light. Even a small flicker would satisfy her need.

I learned today that there are times to defend the weak and times to remain silent. Doctor Maddox told me to be patient. And I will. I have a feeling she will teach me more than medicine.

CHAPTER 7

When Lillian awoke, darkness surrounded her. Was she up before the doctor? She inched onto an elbow. The woman was indeed asleep. Her mind reeled. She couldn't get the boy and his chewed-up leg out of her mind. Was she cut out for this type of healing? She laid back down and curled into a ball and closed her eyes.

She prayed God would protect Vera. And Charlie. And touch Robert's heart. What had made him that way she didn't know. Had he been mistreated as a child? By whom? Her heart sank thinking about how the poor boy felt that day. His fear of his father. Vera's horror. Why had she chosen such a low-down man?

Thankful she was raised in a home with affection, she rolled over. She knew her parents loved her—just not as much as her sister.

She felt tears leaking from her eyes and brushed them away, knowing pity was never the answer. She rolled onto her back, rubbed her arm. When she was certain she would not fall asleep, she crept from her blanket and wandered to the river. Not many animals were stirring this early. Only a few birds chirped.

Sometime later, the rattle of footsteps on leaves and pinecones alerted Lillian to the doctor's arousal. She tossed a couple of rocks in the water and watched the ripples expand. She pretended each ring was someone she would help on her journey. That would be the only way to persevere, to focus on the good. The healing. She wiped her hands on her skirt and made her way to camp.

Doctor Maddox was boiling water. "*Bore da*, good morning. How did you sleep?"

"Well, thank you," Lillian said. "Until this morning."

Doctor Maddox handed her a tin cup. "I heard you stirring. Something on your mind?"

Lillian fingered the cup. "The boy." She dragged in a deep breath. "Truth is, I'm not sure I can handle mangled limbs."

Doctor Maddox nodded. "It took me a few times before some of the worst cases did not bother me."

"You? Like what?"

"I will tell you, but first, why don't you fetch us some tea. I'm sure you snuck some fine herbs in your bag, *le*, yes?"

Lillian smiled. "I have more than tea leaves to share with you." She went for her parfleche.

"I would like to see what you have brought."

The two ladies took part of the morning to share herbs, ideas, and various medicines in the doctor's satchel. By the time they were ready to ride farther north, Lillian's confidence in the journey had been reignited.

A few hours later they came upon a small ranch. Asa's ears twirled from animal to animal: one bull sniffed the air, a few cows chewed their cuds, their calves soaking in the sun, a couple of pigs seemed to hunt for morsels of food, a goat skittered across a pasture, a handful of chickens clucked and pecked, and a cat, crouched, eyeballing one of the chickens. Most of the animals were encased in a few fenced-in areas.

A small pond settled in the back of the property. As Lillian swung a leg over the saddle to dismount, an ear-piercing scream sailed from the small log cabin. Once Doctor Maddox's feet hit the ground, she lifted her skirt and ran. Lillian untied the medical satchel from Chwim's saddle and rushed in after her.

A young woman lay curled in a bed in the one-room log structure, her face red, cradling her rather large abdomen. A fidgety man stood by her side, holding the woman's hand.

"Now Mister Willits, I'm going to need your help."

"Help?" He wiped sweat from his face with a corner of the sheet covering the woman.

He looked as though he would faint. How did Doctor Maddox expect *him* to help? Lillian dropped the satchel on the kitchen table and hurried to Doctor Maddox's side, her gaze on the woman's weathered face.

"What do you want me to do?" Lillian pressed a hand to her neck. The woman cried out, making her cringe. She felt dizzy but managed to remain on her feet.

"Looks like the baby's shoulder is stuck," Doctor Maddox said in a calm tone.

"What?" Jackson Willits said. "How can the child's shoulder be stuck? In there?" He shook his head and wiped his face. "I don't want to know. Do *not* answer me." He dabbed his wife's face with a damp cloth. "Everything's gonna be all right, Sadie. I swear."

Sadie Willits closed her blotched eyes, gripping the sheets with white knuckles.

Lillian put water on to boil. She needed to find a way to accept the things she would have to view and experience. But how? Much of it, like Charlie's leg, she feared was gruesome, other's—screams of pain—churned her stomach. Made her body tremble.

"We're going to need some of those herbs you brought with you, including the witch hazel and vinegar for sterilizing in my satchel. Fetch red raspberry leaf, lemon balm, nettle, red willow, alder, wild rose leaves, and ginger. Also, find a clean sheet or flannel or a small blanket for the baby once he's out. I need a pitcher of wormwood."

Lillian set to work boiling water and collecting supplies.

"He?" Jackson's interest peaked. He gazed at his wife with hopeful eyes.

"Not sure what the little one is," said Doctor Maddox, "don't rightly think I should call the baby an it, do ya?"

"No, ma'am." He shook his head.

Sadie shrieked like a mountain lion and pushed.

"Hold on now, Sadie." Doctor Maddox patted her knee. As time went on, the baby's head continued to turn deeper shades of purple. "We have to get you on your hands and knees." She gazed at Jackson. "In this state, she cannot really hear or comprehend what we are saying. Her mind is on her pain."

"Her what and what?" Jackson wagged his head harder and longer. "Why on earth you gotta do that for?"

Doctor Maddox nodded. "Well, this is going to help Miss Sadie's body adjust so we can deliver this wee one. Now remember, the condition she's in, she's not listening or aware of what we're doing, so we simply need to take hold of her, move her onto the floor, and position her on hands and knees. I can see the baby's head and he's pretty purple. So we need to move quickly."

"Purple?" Jackson said. "Is he dyin'?"

"No, sir, he's not. Let's hurry and get her on the floor, now."

The doctor and Jackson helped Sadie out of bed and positioned her as needed.

Lillian cocked her head as she held up a pouch, felt her eyes widen. *Oh, good Lord, how's this gonna work?*

After Sadie was settled on the floor, her head and neck down to release the infant's shoulder, and several minutes had passed, a baby was born. Cries filled the room, and purple turned to pink. Lillian handed Doctor Maddox squares of flannel, a bowl of boiled wild rose leaves to cleanse the baby with, and a blanket for swaddling.

"Sure enough, Mister Willits, you have a son." Doctor Maddox said. "Would you like to cut the cord?"

Jackson's face went from red to a pale shade of green. "No, ma'am. I'll stay right here with my wife." He rocked back on his heels and blotted his wife's face and then his.

Doctor Maddox smiled. Lillian swore she witnessed the healer chuckle as though tickled about the man's sour reaction to his wife's birthing process. It was more than likely the only time he'd been a part of one. Hopefully not the last.

"Lillian, dear, come on over. You need to learn this part of the birthing process in case there is a time when you need to take over."

Take over? Why would I have to do that? She finished pouring water into a few tin cups and a small pitcher, filled the kettle with water, and placed it back on the cookstove's searing surface. She wondered if she should stoke the stove with wood.

"Come on now." Doctor Maddox waved her over.

47

"Yes, ma'am." Lillian dragged her feet over to the healer's side and took in her learning. Once Sadie and the swaddled babe were settled back in bed, Doctor Maddox began to clean up the area.

Feeling sorry for Jackson, Lillian brought him a chair and a cup of water. He sank into the chair, chugged the water, and asked for more. Lillian obliged.

"Poor fella," Lillian whispered to Doctor Maddox.

"He'll survive. Might even appreciate what his wife has gone through." Doctor Maddox chuckled. "Why don't you go fix the missus some tea. Mix up some red raspberry leaf, lemon balm, nettle, red willow, and alder. That will help her body heal."

Lillian grinned. She enjoyed the healer's spunky sense of humor. "He does seem like a caring man."

"That he is."

Lillian fixed Sadie her tea, pouring more into a jar for later, and helped clean basins, cups, and clothing. By nightfall, everyone was exhausted.

"Feel free to sleep in the barn," Jackson said. "That's all I have to offer."

"That's well enough for us," Doctor Maddox said. "We are thankful for your provisions." She checked on Sadie and the baby.

Through tired eyes, Sadie glanced at the healer and said, "Thank you for saving him." She closed her eyes and yawned.

"He's a fine, strong, *bachgen*, lad. We'll stay on until after breakfast and be on our way." Doctor Maddox brushed a finger over the infant's forehead. "Have you decided on a name?"

Sadie smiled, her eyes still closed. "Henry, after my grandfather."

Doctor Maddox smiled and nodded. "That is a strong name. You get some rest now. Jackson can fetch me if you need help during the night."

Sadie opened her eyes to mere slits. "You're a fine doctor. We need more womenfolk like you in the field."

Doctor Maddox patted her hand. "Sleep well, Missus Willits." She fetched her satchel and herded Lillian to the barn.

CHAPTER 8

Lillian found her journal and pen and wandered over to the pond before turning in for the night. She settled in the grass and stuck her feet in the cool water. A sliver of light lit the pages, enough to scribble her thoughts.

Day three

Not sure I ever want to have children. I'd have to fall deeply in love with a man, and I'm not sure there is one out there for me. Men like Pa are rare. Besides, what if I had complications while birthing?

Never knew a baby could get stuck coming out. And his purple face. All I could do was stand still. I felt if I moved, I'd hit the plank flooring. Never before had I shook like an aspen leaf in a windstorm. Not even when I'd seen little Charlie's mangled leg.

I'm glad the good Lord had sense enough to save Sadie and baby Henry. I still do not think I am suited for this kind of work. But going home is not an option. Not at this time. I have yet to prove myself. Though I may have to find another means. Hopefully, something will arise along the trail.

Doctor Maddox has proven to be a lovely woman with a fine sense of humor. She is the wisest woman I have ever come into contact with. Brave is how I refer to her. I hope to have her courage someday. She inspires those around her. Especially me. She makes me want to keep trying.

I pray there is hope for me.

Lillian closed her book to her chest and fell back into a soft blanket of grass. Stars emerged and twinkled, giving her a sense of wonder. She considered what it would be like to move away, study medicine in a school, and become a certified female doctor. It must be hard taking on a man's name to be accepted by the medical community.

She prayed she would see the day women would be treated as equals.

CHAPTER 9

Lillian woke to the baby's wails. A crack of light poked through the barn doors. She squinted, wondering what it would be like to hold a newborn, one of her flesh and blood, in her arms. The cries muted.

She sat up to find Doctor Maddox gone, suspecting her to be with the new mother. She rose and ambled to the cabin. Even though it was light out, the sun had not yet exposed itself over the eastern mountains. It wouldn't be long. She looked forward to their journey. Giving the couple their privacy. She prayed the next medical crisis would be a broken limb or a slight fever, easily set or taken away with the inner bark of willow.

She opened the door and stepped inside, allowing her eyes to adjust to the dimness of the cabin.

Doctor Maddox looked at her and smiled. "We are going to stay on for a couple of days and help with chores while Mister Willits tends to the animals."

"Oh?" Lillian shut the door. She tried not to let her disappointment show. "Shall I cook the morning meal?"

"That would be lovely." Doctor Maddox said. "Mister Willits will show you where to fetch eggs and

53

whatever else he can offer. You'll find him with the animals."

Lillian nodded and headed back outdoors. She found him feeding the chickens. "Would you like some help, Mister Willits?" The color in his face was back to its tan hue.

"Um—you can gather eggs. My Sadie keeps a basket over there." Jackson pointed to the coop's wall.

"Then if you show me your supplies, I wish to make the morning meal."

He smiled. "That would be fine. Truth be told, my belly's grumbling something fierce. Haven't eaten since yesterday's noon meal."

Lillian gathered eggs and followed Jackson into the cabin. Once flour, salt, milk, butter, sugar, and cream of tartar were gathered, she made biscuits, eggs, and bacon. By the time the food was finished, Jackson came in with fresh milk.

The three of them settled at the small table, Sadie and the baby in bed resting. Jackson scarfed down his food then served his wife her meal in bed. Jackson's tender care over Sadie reminded Lillian of the love between her folks. Only a few days had passed and her desire to flee home was as strong as a ferocious thunderstorm. Torn, she ate her meal in silence, listening to the healer and Jackson go on about caring for Henry, animals, and the impending hot spell.

Lillian rushed through her meal and headed outdoors. The least she could do was to check on the animals. Brush the horses. Learn about pigs and goats, animals she was not raised with, until she was needed for dishes and laundry.

She went to the goat pen. Until now, she had not realized how young the brown and white creature was.

She kneeled beside it, a girl, and rubbed her legs. How splendid to have three colors: white, black, and brown. She ruffled the kid's black and white ears. This little one was charming. And so young. "Where's your mama?" There was no adult in sight. "I bet Sadie named you something cute like Snuggles or Lively." Her mind wandered back to Sadie and her disheveled appearance after giving birth to a baby: sweat-soaked shirtwaist, long brown curls matted to her head, bloodshot eyes. What would have happened if little Henry had lost his mother?

She thought about Doctor Maddox and the healer's wisdom to put the pregnant mother on her hands and knees to save the wedged baby. Lillian had felt good helping with small tasks and was thankful Mali saw her uneasiness and made a divergence for her with the sterilization of instruments and after-care. *I was still learning*…The kid butted her stomach, jolting Lillian from her daydreams.

"Ouch, you little rascal!" She rose, clapping her hands at the critter, and laughed.

A pig in another pen snorted. Lillian strode to their small corral and climbed over the pole fence. Two rather large pink pigs rushed up to her, nosing her skirt. "Ohhh…!" She stepped backward, losing her balance, and fell into the mud. The pig's round snouts rooted her face and arms. She thrashed her arms. "Leave me alone, you scoundrels!"

Strong arms pulled her from them, gathered her mud-caked body into a chest that smelled of sweat and bacon, and over the fence to rest on the hard earth. "You might want to keep your feet planted when Slim and Curly rush ya," Jackson said with a chuckle. "They love people. Heck, Sadie's spoiled every one of 'em." He fanned a muscular, tan arm over the two pens.

"The baby goat, where is his mama?"

"A mountain lion got to her. I used to let the animals roam free until then."

Lillian placed a hand to her neck. "How tragic. She's a cute little thing. I bet Sadie named her too."

"Sure did. Her mama was Rose and that one she calls Pearl."

Lillian giggled. "Pearl. Suits her. What will you do with her?"

"Let her grow into a fine doe, round up a buck, and breed 'em."

"For the milk?"

"Milk and meat."

"You'd eat this little one?" Lillian scrunched her nose. She could never eat such a cute little thing. It would be like eating a fawn. Unheard of!

"Sadie had the same reaction." Jackson wiped his hands on his trousers. "But we wouldn't eat them that young. Only when they were old enough. Now sheep, on the other hand, taste mighty fine when they're young."

Lillian pushed to her feet, shaking her head, and brushed mud from her skirt and shirtwaist. "Best change and start in on the dishes." Her words caught in her throat at the thought of eating any baby animal.

Jackson smiled. "Water's heatin' on the stove."

Lillian nodded. "Much obliged." She gave him a quick wave as she walked to the barn, Jackson's chuckles chased her. *Was he laughing because I fell in the mud or from my reaction to baby goat and sheep meat?* She groaned. A rooster crossed her path. Raised with chickens, she knew this would be no easy task. "Let's get you back to your ladies before a mountain lion gets a hold of you." Crouched over, she tried to herd the brown and black critter toward the cracked-open coop door.

The rooster caught sight of her, swung around and charged her, flapping and pecking her legs. Lillian screamed, batted the rooster, and tried to catch him. He ran, she chased, certain his name was Satan's helper. Then came a hen who clucked and gave chase. Then another. And another.

Deep laughs came from the pigpen. Lillian's face heated, sweat running from her brow. She strode to the coop and opened the door wide. Between her and a gray cat, the chickens and rooster fled to the security of the plank borders they nested in. Lillian slammed the door shut and turned the wooden knob.

The cat flung its tail in the air then rubbed against Lillian's leg. She picked it up and turned face to face. "Thanks for your help, pretty kitty." Clapping sounded in the distance. Jackson stared at her, a sloppy grin on his face, his hands coming together rhythmically. Lillian curtsied, and the cat purred.

"That's Whiskers," Jackson said, "and he knows it's best to herd the chickens rather than kill them. Trust me, Sadie loves the animals and will also protect each one's livelihood. I've never seen someone as gifted around animals as my Sadie."

"She's a fine woman."

Jackson smiled. "Sure is. I'm a lucky fella."

Lillian strode to the barn, closed the door, hugged the cat, and changed into something that did not smell like a horrid mixture of pig and mud.

"How is she?" Lillian asked the healer in a hushed voice.

"She's hotter than bacon in a frypan." Doctor Maddox checked the woman's breathing with her monaural device. "Fetch the stethoscope I gave you and take a listen. Tell me what you hear."

Lillian found her tubular instrument and approached Sadie with caution. Sweat beaded on the woman's forehead, and her face paled. After all that was done to save her life and the life of her son, would she still die?

"Go on now, take a listen."

With light pressure, Lillian leaned over and put the large bell to Sadie's chest and an ivory disc to her own ear. She felt her eyes widen. A rapid swish echoed down the tube. "What is it?"

"Sadie's heartbeat."

Lillian smiled. "The loveliest sound I've ever heard."

"That it is."

"Will she be all right?" Lillian straightened, clutching her stethoscope with tender care.

"I pray so." The healer cocked her head. "What herb do you suggest I give her to reduce the fever, Doctor Gardner?"

"Well, I—I…" Lillian had never been addressed as a doctor before and her mind sank its claws into the title. Could she really become a certified healer? Travel for her education? How far would she have to go? That would certainly be more than "simply a wife," as Hannah put it. She lifted her chin. "Willow bark. A smidgen won't hurt the baby while nursing."

"What about in my satchel? Would any of those herbs work?"

"The only one I'm familiar with is salal. That would also be safe." Lillian felt confident in her answers.

"Very well," Doctor Maddox said. "Why don't you fix Sadie a cup of tea to help ease her fever. You might add lemon balm to calm her and the baby."

"Yes, ma'am. I will." Lillian strode to the kettle and fixed the tea. When cool, she brought it over to Sadie, found her stethoscope, and listened to the woman's breathing. Not much had changed. She kneeled by the doctor, who rocked little Henry.

"Do you think I can attend a university and study medicine?"

"University? Heaven's no. But one of the few institutions to accept women in medicine is the *Woman's Medical College of Pennsylvania*."

Lillian frowned. She couldn't see herself traveling that far away.

"Because there are limited opportunities for women and college, most of the women are self-taught. I will teach you what I know. That will be sufficient, at least for now."

Relief flooded her. Studying under Doctor Maddox would be satisfactory. Or so she hoped.

CHAPTER 10

After the evening meal, Lillian found herself at the pond. She wiggled her toes in the cool water, her journal on her lap.

Day Four

Sadie has spiked a fever and we are staying on for a couple days to help with chores. Doctor Maddox is certain she will be fine. I pray so.

Their animals are an odd sort. Pigs with big flat noses came at me today. They startled me so much I stumbled backward and fell into Mister Willits' embrace. I felt foolish, allowing small animals to get the best of me. And what amusing names—Slim and Curly. Pearl is my favorite. What an adorable little goat.

Tears threaten my eyes when I think of Pearl's mother attacked by the mountain lion. Such a hostile way to die. I would like to have a goat or two when I return home. Whisker's is also a favorite. I think I would like to have a cat that lives in a barn. Mister Willits mentioned they eat mice. Although Sadie has taught the young cat to herd their chickens into the coop. Smart beasts. Or so he claims. I think it was a fluke of sorts.

I think, had Sadie and I met under better circumstances, we would be friends. She and I love animals. We both have named all of ours. Pa does not know, but each bull, cow, and calf have secret names. When I was a little girl, he warned me not to get attached. He specifically told me not to name them as they come and go, some landing on our supper plates. He's right. I know which ones we eat. When they were born and what name I'd given them. But I cannot help myself.

She stopped writing and wiped a tear from her warm cheek. She didn't realize until then how much she missed her father. His encouragement. His smile. His loving embrace. When he called her Lilly Pad and the sound of his voice when he did so. She swirled her toes in the water. Pretending each ripple was a prayer for her father, mother, Hannah and Leslie, and Delbert.

She hugged herself and closed her eyes. A meow came from behind her. Whiskers rubbed against her arm, purring. She picked up the cat and stroked between his ears. "I can do this. I have to finish what I've started."

CHAPTER 11

Four days later Sadie nestled in bed, finally free of fever and gaining strength. With Henry down for a morning nap, Lillian and Doctor Maddox waved to Jackson Willits and headed north.

"When shall we arrive near Kettle Falls?" Lillian tipped her Stetson low over her eyes.

"Soon I believe," Doctor Maddox said. "My orders, or I should say Steffan, my late husband's orders, have been to stay at Meyers Falls community for as long as needed. I have never been there. I expect you have?"

"I was young and do not recall how far it is from here. I do believe you will enjoy the falls, though. We will hear its roar well before seeing the magnificent cascading waters." Lillian inhaled the aroma of pine. Faint wildflower scents drifted in and out as they rode. "Pa told me of the times when Hudson's Bay Fort Colvile was streaming with folks. Both fur traders and Indians. I vaguely recall seeing them one time when Mama let me, Hannah, and Delbert go with Pa to sell his pelts. Before the fort was abandoned. Mama wanted to spend a couple days with Spupaleena and the village healer, so we went with Papa. A child had fallen ill, and she went to help

63

with the siblings and learn more of the herbs Simillkameen used. I have heard of the Meyers Falls community but have not yet been able to visit it."

"You and your *mami*, mother, have much in common then."

A pit formed in Lillian's belly. "Suppose we do."

"You seem to hold ill feelings for her. Mothers are *bendith*, blessings."

"I do not have ill feelings for her, I simply..." Lillian couldn't admit her jealousy out loud.

"I had an older sister once." Doctor Maddox chuckled. "In truth, I have six sisters. I am the second eldest of nine brothers and sisters."

"Nine?"

"My family raised sheep," Doctor Maddox said. "It took all of us to keep the place going."

"Oh my." Lillian thought of Sadie's complications and wondered if Mali's mother had any. "Is your mama still alive?"

"Heavens no. She passed having my youngest sibling—a *merch*, girl."

Lillian bit her lip. That was not the answer she had hoped for. Would she have difficulties birthing a baby? Had her mother?

"This is why I decided to become a doctor."

"Did you attend the *Woman's Medical College of Pennsylvania?*"

"I did not. My husband attended Jefferson Medical College of Philadelphia, and he taught me everything I know. I worked beside him until his death last spring."

"How did he die?" Lillian cleared her throat. "If you don't mind me asking."

"I do not mind." Doctor Maddox gazed at the heavens for a short moment. "He died in his sleep. He

64

had a good life. That evening we had dined with friends near Fort Walla Walla, where we resided. We laughed, rode home, and turned in for the night. I woke up; he did not."

Lillian gasped. "That must have been terrifying."

"It was rather miserable for a time," Doctor Maddox said. "But I am thankful he passed peacefully. Back to your mother. She is the only one you will ever have. By the looks of it, her love for you runs deeper than you realize."

The *clip-clop* of hooves on gravel sounded for a few miles. Lillian thought about all the things she had in common with her mother: stitching, herbs, animals, family. Perhaps the doctor was right. If so, then why had she doted on Hannah all these years?

Hours later, they rounded a corner and came upon flat land among sparse ponderosa pines, several cabins, and a mercantile. Lillian had not expected to see such a structure.

"Shall we stop here and see if they have what we need?" Doctor Maddox reined her horse to a stop and crawled off.

Lillian did the same. "I have no coins and nothing to trade with. Suppose I did not consider I would need anything other than what the land offers."

Doctor Maddox smiled. "When I asked you to join me, I did not presume you would bring much." She lifted a pouch from her saddlebag.

"Still. I should have thought ahead. Forgive me."

"Let's go inside and see what they have to offer."

Lillian followed the doctor into the modest establishment. Lined on shelves or stocked in barrels and crates were canned and dried food, flour, salt, sugar, coffee, fabric, ribbon, spices, and other necessities.

"Can I help you, ladies?" A tall young man said, his gaze going to the doctor's elevated hat. "My name's Jacob Meyers."

Lillian felt heat rise up her neck as the handsome man, seemingly a little older than she, spoke, his gaze fixed on her. She ducked her head, her chest thumping. Her hands trembled, so she tucked them behind her back, pretending to be interested in the jars of candy in front of her on the counter.

Doctor Maddox gave her order to Jacob while Lillian meandered around the crowded post. Jacob talked about his father Louther, the proprietor, how the man after seven years had sent for his wife and sons. How the three of them came from Ontario by way of the Union and Central Pacific railway.

Lillian found herself working her way back to the counter as Jacob talked about his adventure across the British Colombian border, Detroit, and to Walla Walla where he and his family had met up with his father, and the doctor talked about her coming from Wales. He nodded; she smiled. They carried on as if old friends. Lillian found herself pulled to the conversation like a magnet.

"I was nearly fifteen-years-old," he said, his chest puffed out like a self-assured rooster. "We left on October 12, 1869 and landed in the Colville Valley on November 5."

His deep green eyes enticed Lillian. *What an adventure!* His story gave her the courage to finish her own.

"Pa owns the gristmill." Jacob set a head of cabbage on the counter. "We supply all the flour in these parts." He finished gathering her supplies and put them in a flour sack.

"Sounds like your Pa's hard work has done him well."

"Sure has."

"Did you find the flannel, ginger, elixir, and soaps you wanted?"

"*Er mwyn y nefoedd*, for heaven's sake, with all this chatter I plum forgot. *Diolch*, thank you, dear." Doctor Maddox gave Jacob the quantities she needed and browsed items on the counter while he fetched the additional supplies and placed them in another flour sack.

"Can I pack this out for you?" His gaze lingered on Lillian.

Heat rushed up her neck, and her tummy fluttered. She hoped the doctor would agree and let him assist with the supplies.

"I can help the pretty lass," a boy about twenty said as he strode to the counter. "My name's Douglas Maxwell."

Lillian felt the joy dissipate as the blond man tried to push his way through a woman and child browsing a crate of vegetables.

"We can manage but *diolch* for the offer." Doctor Maddox plopped a pouch on the counter and slid it toward Jacob. "This is jerked beef and some coins. I think this will suffice?"

Jacob pushed back the pouch, scowling at Douglas. He then smiled at the healer. "I believe you're the new doctor?" His brow arched.

Doctor Maddox chuckled. "*Le*, I am Doctor Mali Maddox. I need to find out where the clinic is? Can you point me in the right direction?"

Jacob laughed. "There are no clinics in these parts. Although Fort Colville does have military surgeons and a hospital about twelve miles east of here."

"Oh." Doctor Maddox glanced at Lillian. "I suppose we need to figure out where we are to get settled."

The space between Lillian's brow pinched, and she exhaled a disappointed breath. After a moment, she mustered up enough nerve to speak. "Also, can you give us the correct date?"

Jacob gave Lillian a sweet smile. "It's the eleventh of August."

Lillian's chest fluttered. She had never felt so light-headed before as she gazed at the strapping young man, his brown curls wet, sticking to the sides of his neck. "Thank you." She lingered a moment before trying to leave. Douglas stood behind her, his rank breath puffing on her head. She cringed, tried to move to the side, but was blocked by him on her left and Doctor Maddox on the right. She felt pinned. Suffocated. Lillian took a small step toward the healer, praying she'd get the hint to move.

Jacob regarded the doctor. "I believe my pa said there is a house for you. Or for one Steffan Maddox?" Jacob eyed the doctor, a playful grin on his face.

A stout man with a mustache and beard strode into the trading post. "Douglas, what are you doing? Get back to work! And Jacob, the wagon is coming from Fort Colville for flour. They'll need your help loading. Best git, now!" He watched the boy come around the counter. "And it's fourteen cents a pound, not thirteen!" He bellowed.

Douglas smiled at Lillian. "Hope to see you soon, my lady," he whispered close to her ear.

Lillian elbowed him away, her palms sweating.

Jacob nodded. "Yes, sir." He gestured to the healer. "This is Doctor S.M. Maddox and—"

"Do not make them wait, son."

Jacob's face grew red as a beat. He gave Lillian a soft smile and fled outdoors.

The man's eyes grew round. "I—um—well, I was expecting…"

"A man?"

He cleared his throat. "S.M.?"

Doctor Maddox lifted her chin, her shoulders square. "My given name is Mali Maddox. I took on the "S" for my husband Steffan, God rest his soul, in order to carry on his work. I am taking his place now that he is deceased. Now, where are we to set up my clinic?"

"He's dead?" The burly man fingered his beard. "A Clinic?"

"That is correct, Mister…?"

"Louther Meyers." He shook Mali's extended hand. Sweat soaked his white linen shirt, his trousers dusted with flour.

Lillian held in a snicker. She was impressed with Doctor Maddox's brashness. It gave her courage, causing her to straighten her own spine. She took a step closer to get a better view of his whipped expression.

"Our quarters, sir?"

Louther raised a bushy brow. "Our?"

"Forgive me. This is Lillian Gardner." Doctor Maddox winked at the girl. "My assistant."

"You mean midwife."

"No, I mean assistant. She is studying to become a doctor. Is this not wonderful news? Soon there will be many female physicians."

Louther wiped his brow, looking them both over. "A bit young, wouldn't ya say?" He crossed his arms over his stocky chest.

"Perhaps. But she is as keen as a wolf and a delightful healer."

Louther turned to Lillian. "You an orphan?"

Lillian's jaw dropped. "No, sir. My folks live down the river. My father is a rancher."

"Why are you not at home helping your mother?"

Lillian needed that strength she'd seen Doctor Maddox exhibit time and again. She took in a breath, fisted her hands behind her back. "I have my folks' blessing to study medicine. My mother is a healer herself."

"A healer, huh?"

"Yes, she is well-schooled in the medicinal properties of plants. She has even studied under the Sinyekst healer, Simillkameen."

"The who?"

Lillian opened her mouth to further explain, but Doctor Maddox cut in. "Our quarters, Mister Meyers?" She motioned to the door. "We are famished, tired, hot, and dirty. I would like to clean up before seeing patients."

Lillian could tell her charge was madder than a wet barn cat. She chewed her cheeks.

"Yes, ma'am." Louther's face blanched.

"Doctor."

"What?" Louther tipped his head.

"You may refer to me as *Doctor* Maddox." She grabbed her satchel, a few of the supplies, nodded to Lillian, and strode out the door.

Tingles across her arms, Lillian gathered the remainder of the supplies and followed the doctor. She chuckled as she strode by Mister Meyers, enjoying the mix of confusion and upheaval on his face. "Coming?"

He grunted, mumbled something in a strange language to a young gal near the cash register, and stomped behind them. The word "rotzak" buzzed over the counter. Muted giggles whirred from the girl's lips.

70

From the look on his face, Lillian knew it was not a compliment.

Chapter 12

Lillian tossed her parfleche and pouch on a pine chair by a matching table big enough for a couple of books. On it rested a rose-print lantern. The room was the only bedchamber in the ratty cabin. She scratched her head, wondering where she would sleep. In the room stood a tiny single bed with straw poking out of the bed tick and a ratty patchwork quilt. Had they assumed Steffan a small man?

She shook her head and strolled into the main room where it looked like chipmunks had moved in, seeds and debris littered every corner and crevice. In the corner of the room was a cookstove, a few shelves, a worktable, and two chairs. "Where will you put patients?" Lillian had no desire to touch anything.

"We'll have to hang a sheet for privacy in that corner." Doctor Maddox pointed to the side of the house with one window, allowing a hint of light through its dirty pane. She handed Lillian a peeled willow broom. "Best get started."

Thankful corrals were already built and horses were settled in, Lillian brushed dustpan after dustpan of rubble from the plank floor. It didn't take long for sweat to soak her shirtwaist. Doctor Maddox scrubbed the windows and table. When Lillian had finished, she found a washbasin, poured in heated water, found lye soap, and helped scrub anything not nailed down.

Come nightfall, dirt had been beaten from rag-braided rugs and bedding, sheets hung for patient's privacy, an old table lugged in courtesy of Long Nose Louther Meyers for the ill and wounded, and a list made of needed repairs to the cabin, including worn chink sealed between logs.

Lillian fell into a hard chair and sipped from a canteen of cool water. She blotted her warm face with a cool cloth, dreading the close quarters.

Doctor Maddox chewed on a slab of jerked beef. "Suppose we are ready." She patted her neck with her ivory scarf.

Lillian rubbed her stiff fingers. She had not scrubbed a surface like that—ever. Her mother had always kept a tidy cabin, everything wiped down daily and in its place.

"Where shall I sle—"

Jacob burst through the door carrying a screaming child, a frantic woman on his heels. "We need help!"

A weary Doctor Maddox sprang to her feet. "Put him on the table." She pointed to the corner of the cabin. "What happened?"

"My boys—horseplay. I turned my back for a moment and heard this one squallin'. Seems he fell into the cookstove."

"You did not see him?" Doctor Maddox pushed Jacob out of the way. Peeled back charred fabric from the shoulder of his shirt.

The woman shook her head.

"*Os gwellwch yn dda*, please, go to the table and wait." Doctor Maddox pulled the curtain. "Lillian, come here!"

74

Her hands trembling, Lillian grabbed the satchel and went behind the sheet. "How can I help?"

"When we have a patient, do not linger in fear, huddled in a corner. If you want to be a doctor, you must snap to my side."

"Yes, ma'am." She prayed Jacob was not listening.

"Fetch me chloroform, morphine, and sumac." Doctor Maddox glanced at the curtain. "Jacob, light the lantern and bring it to me."

Lillian riffled through the satchel and found what was requested while Doctor Maddox finished peeling fabric from charred flesh. She held a cloth soaked in chloroform over the child's mouth. Shallow breaths expanded her lungs, her stomach lurching from the odor of scorched skin and black muscle. Doubts rushed her like the falls edging the community. If she could not learn to handle what she saw and smelled, how would she ever become a doctor?

Once the boy fell asleep, Doctor Maddox dressed the wound. "I need my stethoscope."

Lillian handed her the instrument and covered her mouth.

"Listen." Doctor Maddox gestured to the boy.

Lillian held out a hand for the stethoscope.

"Where is yours? And your pouch of medicine?" Doctor Maddox scowled, shaking her head.

Lillian rushed through the curtain, past Jacob and the woman, their eyes questioning, gathered her supplies, and hurried to the boy. She slipped her instrument from the pouch, knocking it to the floor, spilling herbs, and pressed the bell of the tube to the child's chest. She eased away, her ear aching.

"What do you hear?"

"A rhythmic whooshing."

Doctor Maddox smiled. "Very good. He is settled and calm."

Lillian stood erect. She wanted to smile but feared the healer would not take her seriously.

"What do you suggest for the burn?" Doctor Maddox said. "From your bag?"

Lillian gathered the buckskin bag and two pouches that had spilled their contents, kicking the scattered bits under the table so no one would slip and fall, and pulled out a handful of small pouches. "Buckbrush, alumroot, plantain, and sumac leaves."

"You have buckbrush? I do not recall you mentioning it in our previous conversations."

"There is some near the river. I can collect the bark and dry and crush it into powder for tomorrow."

"Hand me what you have. I will bandage his arm and shoulder while you go and collect the buckbrush while you still have light."

Lillian nodded, tucked the unused pouches in the bag, and turned to leave."

"Take young Jacob with you." Doctor Maddox fumbled with the pouches. "A woman should never go out this late without an escort."

Lillian froze.

"Is there something else?"

"Jacob?"

"I trust him." Doctor Maddox nodded to the door. "Now go."

Lillian slipped from the curtain and went to the waiting mother. "He will be fine. Doctor Maddox is dressing his arm."

The woman stood and hugged Lillian. "Thank the Lord!"

"That is fine news, Katherine." Jacob pushed to his feet. He blinked several times. Wiped his brow.

"Wait here, ma'am. I…" Jacob took a step toward Lillian causing her to stiffen then she continued. "I will go and collect some bark to help your son heal." Doctor Maddox's shadow danced through the partition. She turned to Jacob. "She wishes for you to escort me."

Jacob swallowed. "Fine."

Lillian fetched her knife and headed out the door, her chest thumping so hard she thought it would burst.

Lillian pulled a knife from its buckskin sheath and sliced a branch from a buckbrush shrub near the plunging falls. "Thank you for escorting me." She laid the branch on the ground.

"I've got nothing better to do." Jacob pulled a blade of grass from the moist earth and slid it between his teeth.

Lillian's heart sank. "Oh…" She cut another branch with a bit more force this time. Tapped it against her skirt. "What do you do for entertainment?"

"Several years ago I planted fruit trees. I enjoy tending to my orchard."

"Sounds lovely. Where is this orchard of yours?"

"Up there." He pointed toward his family's home. "East of our cabin."

Lillian figured he was either a greenhorn when it came to girls or he had no interest in her. Then why had his gaze dawdled on her in the trading post? "Have they bore fruit yet?"

"I have peaches. In another year there will be cherries. A few more after that will come apples, if not sooner."

Shadows crept up the bush as Lillian cut a couple more branches and laid them on the ground. "How will you sell them, from your father's store?"

"What are you two doing way out here with no chaperone?" Douglas said, a twisted smile on his face.

"I'm here to protect her," Jacob said, "from crowbait like you."

"Is that so?" Douglas picked up one of her willow branches and waved it around.

Lillian turned her back on him. "Your orchard sounds lovely. So, what is your plan to sell the fruit?"

"You were correct, at my father's store," Jacob said, a shrill of arrogance in his tone, his gaze darting between Douglas and Lillian. "Once the trees are mature, we will become partners. I plan to supply Fort Colville and Pinckney City with its yield."

Douglas grunted. "Heck, even the Indians are willing to trade for them sweet peaches now they've been shoved on the reservation where they belong."

Lillian stiffened, her pulse racing. "Where they belong?"

"Yeah." Douglas tossed the branch on the ground. "They get drunk off spirits, fight, and steal. Now that they're contained, they should start behavin' like civilized folks."

"Civilized?" Lillian squeezed her knife, fighting the urge to stab his tongue. "The Sinyekst have never touched spirits. They are my family and I will *not* have you speak of them in such a vicious light." She picked up her branches and skirt and rushed back to the clinic.

What a brute! How could Douglas think caging humans on a piece of land is favorable? Even the fort did not allow any type of alcoholic beverages, let alone spirits. The Indians in these parts had always been peaceful. Helpful. Kind. There was no reason not to share the land. Her heart pounded in her chest. *We should all be able to live freely. Unless their name is Douglas Maxwell. He is the one who should be behind bars!*

She stormed into the clinic and slammed the wooden door shut. Then opened it back up due to the stifling heat suffocating the cabin. Setting the branches on the worktable, she searched for something heavy to pound with. There was nothing useful, so she fumed outdoors, found a sizeable stone, marched back inside, peeled the bark from the branch with her knife, the one she should have cut out his tongue with, and began pounding the wood fibers.

"Something bothering you, *annwyl*, dear?"

"Oh, he is a vulgar man!" Lillian pounded harder. Then a soft touch covered her arm.

"You will beat the branch to death soon if you do not settle yourself," Doctor Maddox said. "Why don't you sit and tell me what happened. Was Jacob inappropriate? Was it a dreadful idea for me to send him with you?" Worry creased her forehead.

Lillian wiped her warm brow with the back of her hand and took a seat. "Oh, it was not Jacob. He was lovely to visit with and was a gentleman." She shook her head, her lips pursed. "It was that rotten Douglas. He called the Indians drunken thieves and claimed they deserved to be on reservations."

"That is something to be distressed over." Doctor Maddox lifted a brow. "I wonder where or from whom he formed his narrow opinions."

"I have no inkling. But I promise you this, I will not allow him to speak lies against my family and their people!" Lillian hopped up from the chair and returned to pounding the buckbrush branches.

CHAPTER 13

August 11

Now that Lillian knew the date, she jotted it at the top of a clean page in her journal.

She carved a notch in the strap of her pouch she used to mark the number of days she'd been gone. It had been a week since she'd left home. And it wasn't much easier. She longed for the days riding herd with her father and Jack. Planning the garden with her mother. Collecting and drying medicinal plants and journaling their uses. Which gave her an idea.

On a clean sheet of paper, she listed the herbs she'd used and the medicines Doctor Maddox had used and their purposes. Then added:

It has been a long, weary day. We traveled a good part of the morning then set up the clinic before nightfall. The cabin was a filthy, varmint-infested mess! We managed to clean up the place with empty stomachs. We had a couple of small meals, but with the cookstove in disarray, we could not prepare a proper supper.

When all was complete and we'd hoped to retire for the evening, Jacob rushed in with a boy who had burned his arm. A rambunctious youngster from what his mother implied. Nevertheless, we treated him, after Doctor Maddox scolded me for being ill-prepared. I suppose she was correct in her judgment.

I do, however, appreciate her asking me what herbs and plants I would find useful. If I could only learn to stomach what I see and smell.

Lillian yawned. It had long been dark and her eyes were growing heavy. She sat back in her chair, still fuming over Douglas' opinions about her Sinyekst family.

Jacob Meyers is as charming as I'd hoped he would be. So kind and gracious. I think we will be grand friends, and he will be someone my age I can talk with. I do hope he will introduce me to some other lady friends of his.

Then there is Douglas Maxwell. I dislike him with every breath in me. Once he shared his dislike of "drunk, thieving Indians who deserve to be on reservations," I had no desire to befriend him. Or the likes of anyone with similar beliefs. I cannot help but wonder how many others share his views? Surely not many in this territory. I had not heard of any ill-will among the local Indians and homesteaders.

Lillian shook her fountain pen, wishing she had her old dip writing utensil and ink bowl, not the new style with the internal ink reservoir. She tried to scribble in her journal and shook the pen again as no ink appeared on the page. She slumped in a chair, a dim light casting her shadow on the pages. She tried one more time. Still no ink emerged. She groaned, rubbed her eyes, and closed the journal.

She hoped she could avoid Douglas, but with him working for Louther Meyers, she feared she would not be able to avoid him. In the morning she would have to trade for a new pen or pencils. And there were no guarantees Jacob would be there to assist her.

She let out a ragged sigh. *Tomorrow will be a new day.*

CHAPTER 14

Dawn came early, spilling shards of light into Lillian's eyes. The cabin felt like a dehydrated sweat lodge. Her soggy nightdress clung to her sticky skin. She sat up, her bones groaning. One thin blanket on a wooden floor in the main room was not sufficient cushion. She needed a new bed tick along with ink for her fountain pen.

Sleeping on the floor was not the issue. Its hardness on her bony hips was.

She needed something to trade. But what? She had no food. Doctor Maddox would club her if she traded her stethoscope. Besides, it was the only instrument she had. And she was not about to leech off her companion— even if she'd offered support.

The bedchamber door creaked open. Doctor Maddox padded into the room where Lillian had slept. "You awake, *annwyl*, dear?"

Lillian pushed to her feet and swept up the blankets. "I am. Give me a minute and I'll light the cookstove and boil water for tea." She scurried to the outdoor privy, did her business, and gathered moss, sticks, and pinecones. When inside, she shoved her pickings into the stove, struck a lucifer against the side of the cast iron, and tossed it in with a handful of crisp moss and pine needles. Once a blaze was going, she set a kettle of water on and went to dress behind the curtain, dreading the added heat to the already stifling space.

Her pouches of herbs lay single file on the patient bed. Had she left them that way? Too tired to put them back? She shook her head and gathered the pouches. As she tucked them back into her buckskin bag, a thought concerning a possible trade came to her.

"Lillian, do you have the bark ready for young William?

She tipped her head. "Who?"

"Katherine's son, William."

"Oh, yes. I never knew his name. I'll fetch it for you in a moment." Lillian finished tucking the small pouches in her bag and collected the buckbrush bark powder. "Here it is." She handed the healer a square scrap of flannel.

Doctor Maddox sniffed the bark. "Well done. It is fine and lots of it." She chuckled. "At least you put your anger to good use. Remember, we must leave a legacy of gentleness as well as hope."

Heat flushed Lillian's cheeks. "I suppose so."

"After we have a bite to eat, we can take this to the boy then stop at the trading post. Now that we are finally settled, there are a few things I find I've forgotten." Doctor Maddox patted Lillian's shoulder.

Lillian swallowed hard. "There are a couple of things I need—"

"And I have plenty to trade. Shall we...?" Doctor Maddox waved Lillian on.

Lillian cleared her throat. "If you don't mind, I would prefer to use my own items to trade."

"Oh? Do you have something in mind?" Doctor Maddox held a hand to the doorjamb as if to steady weary legs. She had a pleasing look about her, which should have made it easy for Lillian to speak with confidence.

"Well, I—I saw herbs are limited in the mercantile, so I would like to make a list of what they have and what I could search for and find in the area. It would benefit them and..." Lillian scratched her neck, struggling to find the right words.

"What is it?"

"It just—well—um—I–I believe I need to make my own way. Not rely on you or anyone to provide for me. Like you said, I am now a woman."

Doctor Maddox beamed. "That you are."

"No offense to you, Doctor."

"None taken. And *er mwyn y nefoedd*, for heaven's sake, call me Mali. We're companions, after all. You're not my patient." Doctor Maddox pointed to the door. "Now, let's gather our supplies."

Doctor Maddox, Mali, always made Lillian feel like she could be as free as the wind. "Were we going to eat first?"

The healer chuckled. "I suppose that would be a fine idea."

Forty-Five minutes later, Lillian followed the doctor into the trading post. She prayed Douglas Maxwell would be gone. She rushed to the herbs and got out her journal and pen. She slid the nib of her pen across a blank journal page and no ink rolled out. She shook it and groaned. "Stubborn pen!" she said in a hushed voice.

"Can I help you, lass?"

Lillian recognized Douglas' voice. Her toes curled inside her scuffed boots. She had hoped to avoid the sidewinder but needed ink and a new bed tick. Another night on the floor and she feared she'd be stiffer and bruised. She slowly turned around. "I am in need of a couple of items."

"Have you come down with an ailment?" Douglas' sassy smile turned into furrowed brows, and he leaned forward. Too close.

Lillian turned her face away and took a step backward, bumping into a crate of potatoes. "I am. I mean, yes, I think—an ailment?"

With a swift motion, Douglas righted the crate, gathered the few potatoes that had spilled onto the floor, and gave her a small smile. "You *are* ill then?"

Lillian gasped, heat burning her ears. "No, I mean, oh, everything has gone catawampus!" She smoothed her green skirt with a free hand.

Douglas shifted his weight and raised a brow, leaning in. "Catawampus?"

Lillian sighed, a hand out to halt him from getting closer. "I need either a new fountain pen or pencils and a bed tick—"

"Bed tick?"

"Yes, the floor in the clinic is anything but comfortable—"

"The floor?" His brows lifted.

"Yes, and if you quit interrupting me, I'll finish telling you my plan—"

"Plan?" He crossed his arms, a hint of a smile on his face.

She scowled. "Yes, my plan. As I was saying…" She waited a moment to see if he'd interrupt again. "I need those items and the only thing I have to trade is knowledge—"

He chuckled. "Knowledge, huh?"

Lillian narrowed her eyes. "Yes." She remembered Doctor Maddox's posture in such situations and lengthened her spine, her chin up. "Knowledge in medicine and herbs. Where is Jacob?"

"He's not here at the moment. But I am happy to assist you."

"When will he return?" Lillian hoped he would be back soon.

"He's away for a few days."

Lillian sighed, her insides knotting. The bed tick could wait, but not the pencil. "And where is Mister Louther Meyers?"

"With his son." Douglas gave her a crooked smile.

The back of Lillian's neck felt like a July night filled with the charge of lightning. She mustered the nerve to go on and not let the brute intimidate her. "Seems you have a limited supply. I can help line these rather bare shelves." She tipped her head.

"I see." Douglas studied the jars of herbs. "First I must—"

"Is this a fair barter or not, Mister Maxwell?"

A slow grin bloomed on his face and in a whisper said, "Who is interrupting now?"

She tapped the toe of her boot. "Your answer, please."

"All right then, yes, it is a fair barter. Collect, dry, and contain your herbs and we'll go from there." He turned and took a step.

"Wait!" She hated him acting like the shopkeeper, fearing if they made this deal, Louther might retract it.

He studied her over her shoulder.

She wagged the pen in front of her. "I need a new writing utensil to make my list."

"Suppose you do. I will fetch you one pencil in trade for a single answer to one simple question."

Lillian chewed on her bottom lip. "Go on."

"This afternoon, will you so kindly go on a picnic with me? I will supply the food, basket, beverages, and quilt."

Her face flushed. Inside she groaned. He was nothing but a swindler. But how could she say no? She needed the pencil. "Fine. For one pencil. But that is all. I will wait for Jacob or Mister Meyers to return for the rest."

Douglas nodded and fetched the pencil. "I will pick you up after I load the flour sacks on the fort's wagons. He spun around and strutted out of the trading post like a bull in a corral of heifers.

How could she go on a picnic with an Indian-hater and not kill him? Where was Jacob to escort her? It was him she'd rather dine with. She sighed. *One time.* Then she would be rid of him.

Lillian situated herself overlooking the falls while Douglas spread a colorful quilt on a grassy spot near the edge of the river. He set the basket on the coverlet, sat down, his legs outstretched, and patted a square next to him. She said a quick prayer of self-control and joined him, although not as close as he'd suggested. He pulled from the basket fresh bread, cheese, apples, white meat, and lemonade.

He closed the lid. "The rest is for later."

"And what is this?" Lillian picked up the white meat, praying it had not been poisoned.

"Turkey. I cooked it myself. Shot it this morning, so it's fresh." Douglas motioned for her to take a bite. "Try it."

Not hungry, she tore off a piece and placed it in her mouth. "Mmm." She nodded. Perhaps if she kept him talking, she could find out why he was so bitter toward Indians.

"It's my special recipe."

She tipped her head, forcing herself to play along. "How did you cook it?"

"Perhaps someday I might tell you, but not today." He winked at her and took a bite.

Lillian peeled off a thin strip and handed the rest to Douglas. She put the meat and a slice of cheese on bread and took a bite.

"Hope I can see more of you." He grinned and sank his teeth into another bite of turkey.

His suggestion caused her to choke, her hand patting her chest. "Are there glasses for the lemonade?"

"Apologies, my lady. Allow me." He poured them both the golden drink, lifted his glass in a nod, and sipped, his gaze lingering on her.

She swallowed, cleared her throat, and took a sip, thinking she should have smelled it first. "This is refreshing. Thank you."

"What I was trying to tell you in the store was…" He cleared his throat, sweat beading on his forehead. "I meant no disrespect talking about the Indians like I had before. It was wrong of me. Please accept my apologies."

Lillian wished she could but feared it was too late. She studied his blue eyes and his round face for a spec of sincerity. Even so, why say such perverse things if he didn't mean them? "But why, Douglas? Why would you say such hateful things about my Sinyekst family and other Indians?"

"That's what I don't understand. How are *they* your family?"

She did *not* like the way he said "they" and shook her head. She set her glass down. "Perhaps I need to go back to the clinic."

"What did I do wrong? Do I not have a right to my own opinions?"

"Of course you have the right, as do I, and I do not think your apology is sincere." Lillian pushed to her feet. Douglas did as well and caught her arm, holding tighter than needed.

"You can't be serious about those ruffians being your family."

Ruffians? She was right. His sour outlook shined right through his ignorance. "Does it really matter how? They simply are. That should be enough. I don't know why you are so bitter toward them. Anyhow, I cannot see you aside from the mercantile ever again. I will not entertain the likes of you." Lillian lifted her skirts and dashed toward the clinic.

CHAPTER 15

"Not sure the picnic was worth the pencil!" Lillian checked off another herb from her list. She still needed: plantain, willow bark, alumroot, and red raspberry leaf. She was having trouble locating alumroot and hoped she would not have to travel far to find it.

If she did, she certainly would not ask Douglas to escort her. She'd rather get word to Pekam, her Sinyekst brother. He was always giving, kind, helpful. He understood her more than Spupaleena ever had. She loved her Indian sister, but Hannah and Spupaleena had an unshakable bond. There wasn't much room for another in the mix.

"What did he say to offend you this time?"

"He has the same despicable attitude toward Indians. I'm sure nothing has been done to him or his family. Indians in these parts are peaceful. I just don't understand his hate."

"I did notice there were many..." Doctor Maddox turned a palm to the heavens. "How do you say their name?"

"Sinyekst. Pa says that translates into Bull Trout or Speckled Fish."

91

"That is it. A beautiful name. I noticed there were a number of them at the wedding."

Lillian nodded. "Our families have been close for many years. When Mama was carrying Hannah, Pa found Spupaleena. The day before there was a dreadful winter storm. He had been out setting his traps and found her rather far from the village which is across the river and north of our ranch."

"I believe I saw it from this side."

"That was it. Pa brought her to the old cabin, and Mama fixed her right up. They became like sisters. Spupaleena even had to help deliver Hannah. Pa was gone…" She fiddled with her fingers. "Auntie Spup was nearly my age at the time. Over the years, our families have grown close. Growing up we spent days at a time visiting over there or they'd come stay with us."

"Where was your *dadi*, father, when your sister was born?"

Lillian set her pencil inside the journal and closed the book. "He was in this area. Some bandits attacked him and his friend. Killed his friend and left Pa for dead. Some mountain man—I believe they called him Bunker—got him to Doctor Finlay and came and told Mama and Auntie. Several months had passed by then. That's when our neighbor, Jack Dalley, you met him at the wedding…"

"Mmm." Doctor Maddox said. "The leggy cowboy. Such a gentleman."

Lillian chuckled. "He *can* be a gentleman, and he can be one tough bronco when he wants to be. But it's always for everyone's benefit."

The ladies laughed. "Is that what happened to your *dadi's* leg?" Doctor Maddox brows pinched.

"It is. They say the thug who beat him and stole his traps and tools mangled his leg.

Kind of like little Charlie's but worse." Lillian shuddered. She could not fathom the pain her father had gone through. She was thankful he'd had the will to live.

"Your *dadi* is a strong man." Doctor Maddox fingered her cup. "He had a tremendous will to live. He must love you all deeply."

"That he does," Lillian said, a crack in her voice.

A young girl about ten burst through the clinic door. "Help, please." She waved them over. "Hurry!"

Lillian sprang to her feet. "I'll grab the satchel."

Doctor Maddox pushed to her feet. "What happened?" she asked the dark-haired, dark-eyed girl.

The girl shook her head, growing pale, waved them forward, and rushed out the door.

"Go! I'll catch up." Lillian found the satchel and her buckskin bag and hurried after them. She ran north up a knoll, passing Doctor Maddox, who told her to keep going, swerved southeast and headed downhill for a small cabin surrounded by several cows and a few horses.

The girl glanced over her shoulder, seeming to make sure Lillian was behind her, turned around and sped up.

Lillian's burning lungs fought to take in oxygen, her legs aching. She slowed down, keeping the girl in sight. It wasn't long before the girl disappeared into a log barn. Lillian rounded the corner, entered the barn and stopped. She waited a moment for her eyes to adjust. Panting, she bent over and rested her hands on her legs. "Go find Doctor Maddox and make sure she gets here." Even though her eyes had not adjusted to the darkness, Lillian knew the girl was still in the barn. A shadow raced past her, brushing her skirt.

When Lillian could see figures, she crept forward. On the ground lay a large man, dark red liquid pooling around him. His body quivered, and the smell of blood whirled inside the structure. She held her stomach, holding in a scream. Once she found her bearings, she rushed to his side and kneeled, feeling the warm liquid creep through her skirt.

The smell of aged manure mugged her senses, so she breathed through her mouth. "M—my name is Lillian. I work with Doctor Maddox. She's on the way. Can you tell me what happened?"

He opened his mouth to speak, but no words came out. His eyes squeezed shut as the grip on his leg seemed to tighten, knuckles white. Lillian gently removed his hands with her trembling ones and peeled his torn trousers away from the wound. Blood spilled from a deep gape. She closed her eyes. Bile burned her throat.

"I'm going to try to stop the bleeding," Lillian said, her voice shaky. She wiped her bloody fingers on her skirt, opened the satchel, rummaged through instruments and medication until she found a roll of flannel, and tore off a piece with her teeth. She took the flannel and pressed it against the wound, causing the man to cry out.

"Eek!" She jerked and dropped the flannel into the red mud. The man gritted his teeth, his face red. "Stay with me, mister." She quickly tore off another piece and pressed it against the wound. *Where's Mali?* She didn't see anyone coming yet. They should have been there by now. The man's body shook so badly she thought he might pass out.

"H-h-h-orn…" the man said.

"Horn?"

He nodded.

Lillian looked around. Didn't see anything amiss. Outside cows mooed. Then it hit her. "Did a bull gore you?"

"Y-y-yup." His blood-shot eyes rolled from side to side, his body tremors increasing.

"Where is she?" Lillian said under her breath. Two dark shadows came toward them at a steady pace. "They're almost here." With one hand she held pressure, with the other she fumbled for her stethoscope and pressed it firmly against his chest. He groaned. She listened. His instability made it tough to get a good reading.

She closed her eyes and concentrated. "You need to calm down, mister." She took willow bark from her pouch and slid some into his mouth. "Bite down and let the juice do the work. Don't try to chew, you might…" She didn't want to say it. Couldn't.

"How is he doing?" Doctor Maddox said as she tried to catch her breath, the girl by her side.

Lillian gestured toward the girl, and the doctor asked her to feed the chickens. After the girl disappeared, she answered. "He's in bad shape. I think he was stabbed by a horn from one of the bulls."

"He's got some dandies out there." Doctor Maddox said. "Move aside and let me take a gander." When Lillian was out of the way, she ripped the leg of his trousers open and stuck a couple of fingers in to probe the wound. His eyes squeezed shut, a low growl rumbled from deep inside.

Lillian felt woozy and held her chest. The more Doctor Maddox prodded, the louder he shrieked.

"Get him some chloroform, we're gonna need to clean this out and stitch him up."

95

Lillian nodded, stood, weaved from side to side, and ran outside, retching until nothing more came out. Her body shook. As close to home as she was, she was tempted to abandon Mali, find Asa, and gallop home.

"Lillian, I need your help!"

Lillian wiped her mouth and rushed back in. She got the chloroform and a cloth and covered his mouth while the doctor pressed a cloth to his side.

"He's still bleeding heavily," Doctor Maddox said. "Once he's asleep, fix a poultice from your pouch while I clean out the wound." She proceeded to cut the leg of his trousers.

Lillian nodded, feeling his body begin to relax. Once he was under, she collected the herbs. "I'm not sure I can do this."

"Of course you can. Look at you. You're doing it, aren't ya?" Doctor Maddox frowned. "I told you, it takes some getting used to. Don't be so quick to resign. Now, help me pull off his boots and this part of his trousers."

"Pull them off?"

"Only the leg, we'll keep the rest of him covered."

After they wrangled the boot and trouser leg off him, Doctor Maddox threaded her needle and began to stitch, beginning with the deepest layer. "What are you going to put the poultice on?"

"Huh?" Lillian's hand held the dried herbal concoction. "Do you want me to use strips of flannel?"

"Do you have something better in mind?"

"Sometimes we use leaves and buckskin."

"Do you have those supplies?"

Lillian shook her head. "No, ma'am." She laid the herbs on top of her pouch and fetched more flannel from the satchel. By the time she was done cutting a few strips, the wound was ready for the poultice. She laid the herbs on the stitches and wrapped his leg. "How are we going to get him in the house?"

"Did you find out where the missus is?"

"The girl didn't talk when we got here. I didn't think to ask. He was shaking and bleeding all over the ground."

"Go fetch the girl and we'll see what she knows."

CHAPTER 16

Lillian found the frazzled girl huddled in a corner of the cabin, crying. She sank to the floor beside her. "Hi there."

The tanned face peered at Lillian through dingy arms. "Is papa gonna die too?"

Die too? Lillian wondered what the poor girl had been through. Who else had passed away? "No, not at all. He's going to be fine."

The girl smiled, let her guard down a bit.

"My name's Lillian. What's yours?"

"Edith."

"That sure is a pretty name for a pretty girl." Lillian grinned. She felt bad for the scared girl. The child was no more than seven years of age. With no sign of a mother in the cabin, she wondered what had happened. Hopefully, she was not one of those who'd died according to Edith. Who knew? Lillian had noticed their tiny home was littered with dirty dishes and filthy, threadbare clothing. The floor hadn't been swept…well she didn't know how long it'd been. Edith was as grimy as her dress, her matted short hair disheveled.

Edith gave her a small smile in return.

"What is your pa's name?"

Edith's eyes grew wide. "Papa."

Lillian pressed her lips together. She thought by now the girl would have known her own father's name.

"Where's your mama?"

Tears welled in the girl's eyes, and she dropped her chin. "Out back."

So she was alive. Feeling hopeful, Lillian stood. "Will you show me?"

Edith nodded. She sniffed, wiped her face with the sleeve of her dress and went to the door. Lillian followed the girl to the back of the house. They stopped under a grove of quaking aspen. At the base of the trees were five wooden headstones which in carved letters read: Ida Lawson, baby boy, baby boy, baby girl, baby boy. There were no dates or names for the children.

By the looks of it, Ida had died last winter.

She figured the man's surname had to be Lawson.

Lillian's heart ached for Edith and her father. She didn't know what to do. Take the girl to Doctor Maddox and her father? Wash her up and change her dress? She had to be traumatized by it all.

"Are you hungry?"

Edith nodded, wiping tears from her eyes.

When had she last eaten? Lillian held out her hand, and Edith looked away. Lillian slid her hand in the small one and gave her a gentle squeeze. "Let's get some food in your tummy, wash you up, then I'll take you to see your pa."

Once inside the modest cabin, Lillian set the girl at the table, cleared dirty dishes, and found a few eggs and potatoes to fry. She wished she could toss an onion in but hadn't found any. While the food sizzled in lard, she set water on for coffee as there was no tea. "Do you have any milk?"

"I went to milk this morning, but the blasted cow kept kicking the pale," she said in a quiet tone. "Couldn't find Pa, so I collected those eggs."

"Do you know what happened to your pa?" Lillian flipped the eggs.

Doctor Maddox stepped inside the cabin, glanced around, and settled at the table opposite of Edith. The girl watched the old woman shuffle around from the inner side of thick lashes.

"He came back from checkin' the cattle holding his leg, hollerin' for me to fetch help. I ran as fast as I could. You were the first ones I found home." Edith stared at the doctor.

"I'm Doctor Maddox," Mali said. "We fixed your pa up and we'll bring him inside soon. He's resting for a bit first." She leaned forward and tilted her head as she peered at Lillian.

"This is Edith. I don't think she's eaten much today, so I thought it best to fix her a little something."

"Fine idea." Doctor Maddox turned to Edith. "Do you have a cup of water? My mouth is parched. And I'm old. It was quite the jaunt for me to get here." She winked at the girl.

"I can fetch you a cup from the barrel on the back porch."

"That would be lovely."

Lillian handed Edith a cup, and the girl scurried outside.

"What did you find out about the mother?" Doctor Maddox wet her cracked lips.

"Edith took me to see her."

Doctor Maddox leaned forward, her brows lifted. "Oh?"

"She's out back with four babies."

101

"Four?"

"In a graveyard." Lillian found a clean plate and scooped on eggs and potatoes. "The poor dear is distressed. She doesn't even know her father's name." Lillian set the plate on the table where Edith had been sitting.

"She doesn't? How odd."

"That's what I thought."

Edith carefully walked the cup to Doctor Maddox. "Why *diolch*, Edith."

Edith smiled and took her seat. She ate like a famished weasel. When done she wiped her mouth with the back of her hand. Lillian caught the doctor's gaze and smiled.

"Let's clean you up and then we'll take you to see your pa."

Edith stiffened when Lillian placed a hand on her bony shoulder.

"What's wrong?"

Tears pooled in the girl's eyes. "I'm scared."

"You're safe with us." Lillian kneeled beside her. "You can rest in here and we'll fetch your pa. How does that sound?"

Edith nodded, picked up a ratty doll off the floor, and settled in a rickety-old blue stuffed chair. Doctor Maddox took a drink of water and passed the cup to Lillian. She drank the rest of it and plunked the cup on the table. The women made their way down the wobbly porch stairs and to the barn.

"How are we going to move him? He's a rather large fellow." Lillian furrowed her brows.

"If we can roll him onto a blanket, we can drag him to the steps." Doctor Maddox jerked a thumb back toward the cabin.

"And then what?" Lillian stopped and faced the healer.

From the entrance to the barn, Doctor Maddox studied the still form on the ground and the steps. "Perhaps you should go fetch Jacob and his friend."

"Douglas?" Lillian cringed. "I will find someone else."

"No matter," Doctor Maddox said. "Just find a couple of strong men. I'll keep the girl company." She turned and hobbled toward the cabin.

Lillian groaned and headed for the clinic. *I'll bring Asa and Chwim back with me. And the canteen. Apples and jerked meat.* Lillian's stomach growled. The sun beat down on her head as she walked. She'd need to gather their hats. As she walked, she thought about what needed to be done and gathered, about Edith and what the dear girl had been through, how Ida and the babies may have died, how old they'd been, about how Mister Lawson could have possibly been gored—

"What's your hurry?" Douglas smiled, slipping a long blade of grass from his mouth.

Lillian kept walking, pretending she hadn't noticed his presence leaning against a thin aspen. She could not—would not—carry on with a discriminatory sidewinder such as Douglas Maxwell.

He caught up with Lillian and strode alongside her. "I suppose I owe you another apology."

"You won't mean it."

He grabbed her arm and twirled her around.

"Ouch!" Lillian tried to jerk her arm away, but he held tightly. "Let go!"

He pulled her into his arms and tried to kiss her. She slapped him in the face, kneed him, and sprinted toward town.

"Stay away from me!" she hollered over her shoulder. She rushed to the clinic, gathered the supplies, saddled the horses, tied them to a post, and went in search of help. Not knowing where to go, she hurried to the livery and found a man reclined in a chair in the shade, his hat pulled over his eyes. "I need help!"

He startled awake, his hat flopping to the ground. He picked it up, stood, and dusted it across his leg. "What's the matter?"

"A man that-a-way," she pointed over the hill, "Got himself gored. The doctor and I need help moving him from the barn to his cabin."

The red-headed man towered over Lillian. "I'll fetch us more help and meet you at the clinic."

Lillian nodded, curious as to how he knew about the medical establishment. They'd only been there a day. She lifted her skirt, dashed to the clinic, threw on a split riding skirt, and met the red-head and a stout man in suspenders by the horses. She pressed her Stetson on her head. "Follow me."

"Do we need horses?" the liveryman said. "How far over the hill is it?"

"Not far. The doctor is older and weary. I'm bringing more supplies for us and she could use the horse to get back."

The men nodded and followed Lillian.

She felt flush as they rode, searching for sign of Douglas Maxwell.

At the Lawson ranch Lillian slid off her horse, thankful they had not run into Douglas, and untied a large buckskin pouch from the cantle of her saddle. "I'll fetch the doctor." She stepped inside and found Mali reading a book to Edith. "I found help." She set a bag on a chair, handed Mali her tall hat, and set rations on the table.

"My hat!" Doctor Maddox rose. "*Diolch*. I was wondering how I'd make it home in the heat. She fanned her flush face with the open book.

"Chwim's outside." Lillian handed the healer some jerked venison and dried apples.

"A fine plan. You are a dear." Doctor Maddox took a bite of meat and handed a few slices of apple to Edith. "You stay in here, now. Clear a spot for your pa."

Edith nodded and disappeared into a room.

"How is she?"

"Won't say much, but I think she'll be fine once she sees her father is going to live."

Lillian gestured to the door. "With the two men I rounded up, we won't have to do any heavy lifting."

"A fine job, *annwyl*, dear." She patted Lillian's arm. "My body is long past lifting anything over the size of a small pumpkin."

Lillian winced at the healer's touch.

"*O na wyt ti'n iawn,* oh my, are you alright? Did you fall on the way to the clinic?"

Lillian didn't know if she should alarm the old woman. "I'm fine. They're waiting, shall we go?" She and the men followed Doctor Maddox into the barn. "Looks like he's not moved."

"When I checked on him a while ago," Doctor Maddox said, "he was waking up. He became cantankerous, so I gave him some morphine. He should now sleep for some time."

The red-head turned to his partner. "This is Neil Lawson."

"So you know him?" Doctor Maddox's gaze dropped to Neil.

Red-head nodded. "Helped bury his wife and babies."

"What happened to them?" Lillian tipped her head.

"After the last baby died of the fever," Red-head said, "Ida went crazy. Neil tried to help her, but she wouldn't listen. Couldn't seem to get over the babies' deaths. Edith wasn't enough to live for, I suppose. They quarreled one night, and she ended up in the river. No one knows what all took place, but she drowned and left Neil to raise the girl on his own."

"That happens all too often with women who lose their babies." Doctor Maddox stared at the wounded man as if she knew what it was like to have lost a child. "We best get him inside."

The men lifted Neil, carried him to his bed, and left. Edith stood in the corner, wide-eyed.

Lillian held out a hand to her. "It's all right. Come on over. You can see he's sleeping."

She leaned forward, studied her pa for a moment, and fled the room.

"Oh…" Lillian sighed.

"Give her some time. She'll come around." Doctor Maddox checked his bandages and covered him up with a sheet. "I'll stay with him overnight. Put Chwim up in the barn, scoop the blood out, and head back to the clinic. Edith and I can take care of everything else."

The thought of Douglas lurking around the clinic made Lillian shiver. "Perhaps I should stay."

Doctor Maddox examined Lillian's face. "What happened to you today?"

"Nothing, really—"

"Did you have a run-in with Douglas?"

Lillian hated to lie. But what good would it do to worry the healer too? She had enough on her mind.

Especially if she was going to stay. "If you think I can handle the clinic."

"If calamity arises, you know where to find me. *Nos da*, good night."

Lillian nodded, grabbed the gray, and headed for the barn.

CHAPTER 17

August 12

Lillian spent the rest of the day collecting herbs. After a light supper, she settled under a tall pine to pen her thoughts in her journal.

This has been a most peculiar day. The morning began with Doctor Maddox and me visiting about various medications and their use and young William's treatment. I shared my knowledge of herbs and she her wisdom about the medicines she carries and wishes she had with her. At some point, we will have to travel to Fort Colville and see what the army surgeon has available.

There is a good chance we will have to stay a few nights as some of those medications will have to be ordered and shipped in by stage. We fixed a simple morning meal and headed to the trading post. It felt nice to earn my own way. I had preferred to deal with Jacob and was disheartened to find he was out of the area. Dreadful Douglas was riding herd over the shop.

How I let him talk me into a picnic for a pencil was foolish on my part. I should have waited until Jacob returned. I can see myself marrying someone like Jacob. Kind. Generous. A true gentleman.

My run-in with Douglas was not the worst part of the day. Poor little Edith. She has a special place in my heart. I would raise her as my own if I could. What a sweet child. To watch her father nearly bleed out in the barn, her mother dead. Siblings dead. She's been through enough. Perhaps I should bring the matter to Mali's attention. Only the Lord knows how long it will take Neil Lawson to recover. If infections sets in, he may die. Then what would happen to Edith? Perhaps it's not medicine that is my purpose in life, rather it is taking in orphans.

She and I did bond. And maybe if I keep working at it, she will eventually tell us what really happened to her father. We can only assume he was gored by a bull. When I see Doctor Maddox in the morning, there is a good chance she will have solved the mystery.

For now, I will pray Edith will be protected from further heartache.

CHAPTER 18

Lillian washed the morning dishes, wondering if Jacob had returned and she could talk more with him about trading herbs for a bed tick and fountain pen. Perhaps she would take a few more pencils in case the new pen failed her.

Once a barter was made, she planned on riding to the ranch and checking in on Edith. Perhaps she could trade for fabric and stitch her a new dress. She dried the last of the dishes and put them on the shelf, checked on Asa, and made her way to the trading post.

She smiled as she strode through the door. Jacob was there, taking inventory. Her belly fluttered, and her hands shook. She smoothed her dress with damp fingers and made her way to him. "Good morning."

"If it isn't Miss Lillian, chief herb trader."

Heat rose up Lillian's neck, burning her cheeks. "You must have spoken with Douglas."

"I have. And it is a fine plan. I've already ordered a bed tick for you. Do you have the herbs with you?" With a hand, he gestured her over to the line of jars on an herbal shelf."

"I do." Lillian explained what they lacked and what she could offer.

Jacob nodded. "I agree. These will be a valued addition to our selection. I'll take them all."

Lillian cleared her throat. "I—uh—I also need a new fountain pen or ink, mine isn't working, two pencils and fabric. I want to make a dress for a young girl."

"Pick them out. What you have here is sufficient payment."

Lillian rummaged through various fabrics, settling on a light green floral cotton for the dress and ruffles and white lace for the collar. As she picked up the fabric to carry to the counter, a young woman sauntered it. Her amber hair neatly pinned on the crown of her head, wisps hanging down and framing a soft, round face. Her emerald eyes found Jacob's. He strode to her and held her in a warm embrace.

"Good morning, Jensena. How did you sleep?" A hand lingered on her arm.

"Quite well." Her cheeks pinked. "Your aunt is a gracious host."

Lillian swallowed and placed the fabric on the counter. "I'm ready." Her voice croaked like a toad with laryngitis. She marveled at the woman's lilac satin dress and bustle, appearing ready for a wedding or some other highfalutin social gathering. Lillian fingered her cotton skirt, convincing herself it was a useful garment for her line of work.

"Lillian, I'd like to introduce my bride to you." Jacob's face shined.

Lillian's head swam. "Bride?"

Jensena held out a hand. "It is a pleasure to make your acquaintance." Her voice had a thick Danish accent to it. She stood as poised as one of the east-coast debutantes her mother had told her about.

"The pleasure is mine." Lillian shook her petite hand.

"This is the young healer I was telling you about," Jacob said. "Come, look at the herbs she has collected. She is remarkable."

Yet not so remarkable to choose as a wife. Or even consider! Lillian felt as deprived as Edith looked. But of course, he would choose someone like her. He was a young businessman with a successful orchard. Someday he would take over his father's kingdom, Jensena his queen.

"These look wonderful. You must be a fine healer. Do you travel alone?"

"No," Lillian said, "I'm journeying with Doctor Maddox. She is from Wales and teaching me her ways of medicine and I'm sharing mine with her." Jensena's beauty and poise made her feel inadequate. She felt herself shrinking.

"Marvelous," Jensena said. "Perhaps we can go on a walk this evening. I need more female companions. Jacob cannot take all of my time." She giggled, hanging onto his muscular arms.

Jacob kissed the top of her head, his face beaming. "That is a wonderful idea." He turned to Lillian. "Let me cut this fabric and fetch your writing utensils and you can be on your way."

On my way. And hopefully far from here! Lillian nodded, wetting her parched lips. It was clear they were in love. *Maybe Hannah was right, I'll be nothing more than a caretaker for our folks.* She felt her shoulders droop. Not even the images of a strong female doctor could pull her out of her pity.

Back at the clinic, she gathered a few supplies, saddled Asa, and headed for the Lawson ranch. How could she have been so foolish? To think Jacob was interested in her. Let that be a lesson. Not every kind man is attracted to a simple lady. At least not in the fashion she'd wished for.

And now to think she would have to be companions with Jensena. She shuddered at the thought.

A swift breeze swirled dust into her eyes, so she dropped her chin, pulled her hat low over her brow, and kicked Asa into a lope and shifted her thoughts to Edith. Was the girl still distressed? Had Doctor Maddox seen to giving her and her clothing a good scrubbing?

As she crowned the hill, the scent of cow lingered in the air. Two bulls with sharp horns grazed in the distance. One of them must have been the culprit. Did Neil get caught between them? The valley filled with faded grass the color of crickets and corn stalks. She let Asa gallop to the cabin, feeling the thrill of speed tingle her nerves.

Lillian dismounted, spitting out a whorl of hair caught in her mouth, and tied her gelding to a hitching post. Dirt whipped at her face. With haste, she gathered the supplies and hurried into the cabin. Edith lay curled in a ball, her eyes closed, looking like a dirty cream mint on a peach-colored sofa. Had the girl suffered from nightmares? Lillian could only imagine. She covered Edith with a light coverlet.

And what about Mali? How was she holding up? Lillian poked her head in the room, holding her breath against the stagnant aroma of blood, manure, and man's sweat. Bits of dirt tapped the window, but she didn't care.

She strode to it and struggled to lift, but the sill was stuck. She jiggled and attempted to lift the wood and glass again.

"I already tried," Doctor Maddox said. "It will not budge."

Lillian fanned the air around her nose. "How is he?"

"Not well." Doctor Maddox slumped her shoulders, her eyes puffy. "It has been a long night. His fever has spiked. His breathing is rapid. I have done all I can."

"What now?"

"We need to take him to Fort Colville and see if the surgeon can treat him. I don't have what he needs. This happens when I do not have a proper clinic and appropriate medications."

Lillian went to Neil's side. "How will we get him there? What do we do with Edith?"

"There is a buckboard behind the barn. We'll hitch his horses to it and tie ours to the back. Take the girl with us."

Lillian sighed, her shoulders feeling light. "Has Edith eaten yet?"

"A couple of eggs and old biscuits her father must have made the day before."

"I will bathe her and feed us both." Lillian clasped her hands together. "Then I reckon we'll hitch the buckboard, fetch our belongings, and be on our way?" *Away from Jacob and his bride. And Dreadful Douglas.*

Doctor Maddox tilted her head. "I thought you enjoyed it here. And now it seems you cannot leave quick enough."

Lillian wrung her hands, not wanting to tell Mali about Jensena. "I only wish to get Mister Lawson the help he needs. Edith cannot endure another death."

Doctor Maddox nodded. "*Le,* that is correct."

115

The ladies spent the rest of the morning preparing for their journey. It would be a simple fifteen miles, but if the wind kept its pace, it would be slow and gritty.

Lillian squinted her eyes and handed the reins to Doctor Maddox. "I'll check on Edith. She looks miserable."

Doctor Maddox took the reins, the chestnut pair of workhorses plodding along, their heads down. Lillian crawled over the seat and pulled a quilt over Edith's head to block the wind and dust.

Lillian settled beside the healer. "The cows! We didn't tell anyone to watch over the cows."

Doctor Maddox handed the reins. "While you went to fetch the rest of our supplies, I had a chat with Louther and Jacob. Between them and Douglas, they will oversee the animals."

"They were at the cabin?"

"They'd heard about Mister Lawson's mishap and came to see for themselves."

Lillian stiffened, thankful they were behind them.

"I will post an update in a few days concerning his health."

"Good," Lillian said. "I am sure they will appreciate it."

Doctor Maddox chuckled. "I met Jensena."

Lillian snapped the reins. "Did you now." Why did the woman get under her skin like she did? She and the healer hadn't planned on sticking around anyhow. She shook her head, her gaze fixed on the flat valley ahead.

It was blistering hot when they veered north toward Douglas Falls and Fort Colville. A few miles north a flag soared high above the fort's parade grounds. Tree-covered mountains provided a glorious backdrop against the pole fence enclosing the fort's buildings. Inside the square fence lined structures both small and large. Around forty to fifty soldiers dressed in post-civil war uniforms, some carrying muzzle loading rifles, roamed the area inside the borders. An "L" shaped building stood off to the left, south of the fort.

Lillian pulled the horses to a halt. "Where to, Doctor?"

Edith poked her head from the wagon bed, her eyes wide and searching. She glanced at her father and patted his covered shoulder.

"Louther Meyers said the hospital was the shape of an "L" so let's try that one." Doctor Maddox pointed to the desired building.

Lillian flicked the reins. "Let's go, boys." The chestnuts leaned into their collars and plodded forward. When they came upon the white-washed hewn log hospital, Lillian pulled on the reins and the wagon rolled to a stop. She fixed the brake and took in the structure and its long, uncovered porch.

"I'll fetch the surgeon." Doctor Maddox went to stand when Lillian caught her arm.

"I'll go. You stay with them." Before the healer could argue, Lillian climbed out of the wagon. Once down, she smoothed her skirt and wiped loose strands of hair from her face. She strode to the door, her pulse racing as this was the first time she'd seen a hospital.

She ascended the two steps slowly, her breaths coming at a rapid pace. Her hand reached out to open the door when it flung open and a man in farming attire dashed out, knocking her to the ground. Without a word, he kept going.

Another uniformed man of average build with sandy-brown hair and a mustache reached for her. Lillian took hold of his weathered hand, and he pulled her to her feet.

"Are you all right, Miss?" he said.

Lillian nodded. "I am. Thank you."

"That man was late for—well now, can't rightly go 'round gossiping about my patient can I?"

She brushed dirt from her skirt, thankful the wind had died down. "Reckon not."

His brows pinched as he studied the wagon, the woman with the high hat and flannel attire, and the girl, her eyes peeking from the seat's backrest. "You all travel together?"

"We did." Lillian moved to the buckboard. "May I introduce Doctor Maddox?"

While the surgeon helped the healer out of the wagon and followed her around the back of the bed, Lillian noticed a gruff-looking fella with a black cowboy hat and two six-shooters hanging from wiry hips staring at her, causing a sour taste to form in her mouth. His scruffy beard was in need of a wash and trim, and his clothing and neckerchief looked just as shabby. He tipped the brim of his hat and gave her a toothless grin. She shuddered and turned to face the doctors.

"Call me Mali. This man was gored by a bull, or so we think. His fever spiked last night and has not come down. I do not have the supplies needed to fight the infection that seems to have taken over his body, *Meddyg*, Doctor…?"

"Forgive my rude manners. I'm Doctor Evan Harris." He gave a simple bow to the women in a playful manner.

"Pleasure to know you." She nodded. "This is Miss Lillian Gardner and the girl is Edith, Mister Lawson's daughter—"

"And I'm assuming this chap is Mister Lawson…" He winked at Edith, and she smiled back at him.

Doctor Maddox nodded. "Mister Neil Lawson."

Doctor Harris grew serious as he watched the man wince. "What have you administered to him?"

"Morphine."

He nodded. And when Neil Lawson groaned, said, "Let's get him inside." He reached to pull him closer.

"Do you really think we can lift this size of man up those steps and into your hospital?"

Doctor Harris' gaze darted from Edith, to Lillian, to the healer. "Well, she might." He winked at Edith, making her giggle. "You win." He scuttled into the hospital and came out with a couple of stout men. "We have help!"

The men lifted the bedding Neil lay on and heaved him up the steps and into a room.

Lillian and Edith followed Doctor Maddox and the men. She settled Edith in a chair and found the doctors and Mister Lawson in a cramped room with a bed, a small table, and a few instruments. A small window lit the room. Crimson stained bedding lay heaped on the floor.

"Miss Lillian, if you could wait in the—"

"She is a healer herself and training under my guidance," Doctor Maddox said. "She can remain in the room."

Doctor Harris gave Lillian a thorough once-over and poked a finger in Neil's wound. "I believe you are right.

He was gored by a bull. But there is more damage and I need to get him into surgery right away. Doctor Maddox, would you like to assist?"

Mali nodded. "I would." She turned to Lillian. "Find something for you and Edith to eat."

"I will have our cook fix you both a meal," Doctor Harris said, turning his attention on Doctor Maddox. "You will need to eat a little something also, it will be a few hours—"

"I am fine. Let's get him ready, shall we?"

Doctor Harris nodded.

"Feel free to wait in my office, Doctor Gardner."

"I—"

"Before he wakes up again," Doctor Maddox demanded.

Doctor Harris called for the two men, and Neil was moved into another room. Lillian fetched Edith and roamed the short hallway until she found what looked like an office. She pressed on the door and it creaked open.

A desk leaned against the outer wall next to a window, a chair tucked underneath. An open book rested on the desk near a pen and ink well, journal, and a few pencils. A tin lamp perched on the corner of the desk. Books lined a shelf on one wall, and Lillian strode over, a finger following the spines of a few medical volumes.

She ambled to the desk—to the open text. The pages open were surgical instructions for amputation. She leaned over and thumbed through the book. She felt faint, knowing this is what her father had gone through. She had a sudden admiration for Doctor Finlay and his compassion for her father.

"What are you looking at?" Edith peered at the pages and gasped.

Lillian slammed the text shut.

"There you are!" A robust woman wearing a white cap and apron said. "I fixed you up some fried cabbage, onions, and roasted beef." She beamed at the girls and waved for them to follow. "Come on now."

Edith took hold of Lillian's hand and the girls followed the cook down the hall and into another tiny room with a cookstove; shelves filled with spices, dishes, pots and pans, and utensils; one table; and a handful of chairs. Edith crawled into one chair and Lillian sank into another.

The cook served them their food. "My name's Nettie. Let me know if you need anything else."

Lillian picked at her food as Edith devoured hers. Her mind wandered to her one-legged father. All he'd been through. What a brave man—a survivor. She thought about her mother's love and support of her husband and family. Her fight to find him, clinging to a thread of hope that he was alive. How much grief Hannah had caused. How much time her folks had to invest in her sister in order to keep her safe during her rebellious years.

A cramp of regret grabbed her stomach. Hannah had been a handful concerning shenanigans. Maybe her folks did love her as much. But still, she'd come this far. She'd stick it out until winter threatened then would find her way home. Who knows, there was still time to find herself a fella along the way. She was of the marrying age, after all. And not simply a caretaker.

CHAPTER 19

August 13

I am utterly exhausted. Yet thankful we were able to pitch a tent near the hospital as we are doctors, at least I now pass as one. Captain Miles was kind enough to donate two unused tents so we'd have shelter.

I feel overwhelmed from the day's travel, but overjoyed Neil Lawson will survive. The surgery was a success! I wish I could have attended the procedure to learn another skill. I am confident by now my stomach would not have lurched. I seem to be adjusting to the sights and smells of the profession. Doctor Harris did have me boil the instruments and clean the surgery table, claiming every doctor had to start somewhere, while the cook kept an eye on Edith. That was all right with me because afterward, he allowed me to take a gander at his medical books.

Edith smiled today, even giggled, as she was able to see her father. It showed how pretty she is, her face glowing and all. Tears gathered in my eyes as her little hand held his. Fear seemed to dissipate from her body as she sang to him quietly, her head resting on his chest. Made me miss my pa and his fatherly touch of encouragement and comfort. I am convinced there is a special bond between father and daughter and mother and son. I see the way

123

Mama looks at Delbert when he is working, pride in her eyes. They have a special way about them.

The distractions of the day made me forget about Jacob. It was only when I found quiet time did his rejection tug at my heartstrings. Lord, let me be happy for him and his bride. I can only trust you will have a suitable fella for me when the time is right.

Lillian's eyes grew heavy, and she struggled to keep them open. She rubbed her eyes and yawned.

Tomorrow, after we gather needed supplies and a pack horse, we will journey to the Pend Oreille River Territory. Doctor Harris mentioned the Kalispeli_whos_ do not have a doctor in the area. I remember watching Spupaleena race horses against these folks. She referred to them as the River Paddlers. Men wear abalone earrings. Their attire is similar to the Sinyekst of Spupaleena's village, yet have a unique flair to it, one I find rather attractive.

It will be a long journey, two days at least if not longer as Doctor Maddox seems weary, over a rugged mountain pass on Indian trails. Captain Miles drew a map for us on parchment. The trails look simple enough. By the looks of it, we will head north for a time, drop down into a valley he says in autumn is lit with colors as bright and vivid as a fire on a starless evening, and follow the Pend Oreille River south for several miles until we find a village. I pray they have a healer I can visit with and learn about native plants in their region and their medicinal properties.

Lillian closed her eyes, wanting to pen more into her journal...

Chapter 20

"Missus Simpson is here to collect Edith." Lillian hollered at Doctor Maddox. She was unsure if the healer was still in the tent or went to the privy. She was just here, organizing her medical bag. The tent was empty. Edith was nowhere in sight. "I'll find them," she said to the young woman, an infant in her arms.

She rushed around, trying to locate the missing companions, finding them in the kitchen of the hospital. Doctor Maddox handed her a plate of fried eggs, bacon, biscuits and gravy. "Better fill your belly, we won't get a meal like this to stick to our ribs for some time."

"Missus Simpson is at camp." Lillian nodded to Edith, the girl's back to her.

Doctor Maddox mopped the last of her gravy with a biscuit, plopped it into her mouth, and headed out the door. Lillian sat beside Edith so Mali could talk privately with the woman.

"Missus Simpson seems like a nice lady," Lillian said to Edith. "She has a baby. I bet you'll be a fine helper while your Pa heals. The doctor will have him fixed up in no time and you'll be able to go home."

Edith smiled, her cheeks as full as a chipmunk's and her eyes twinkling like stars. Even the color was back in her face.

"Have you seen him this morning?"

Edith shook her head and swallowed. "Doctor Harris said I can when I'm done eatin'.'"

When they were finished, Lillian took Edith to meet Missus Simpson. Once they were acquainted and Edith seemed relaxed, playing with the baby, she headed back to the clinic to meet Neil Lawson and bid farewell.

She hopped up the steps and went inside. Doctor Harris was in his office, his nose in a book. Lillian knocked.

"Oh, Doctor Gardner, come in." He waved Lillian over. "I suppose you ladies are getting ready to hit the trail."

"Yes, sir, Doc—"

"No need for formalities, we are colleagues, are we not?" Doctor Harris tipped his head. "Have you seen the patient this morning?"

"That's why I'm here. I'd like to actually meet Mister Lawson before we, as you say, hit the trail."

"That's the spirit!" Doctor Harris sprang to his feet and in a few long strides made it to the door. "Come along, now, I'll be delighted to introduce you. He's a rather charming chap, if you don't mind me saying so."

Lillian followed him into Neil's room. He appeared weak, but much healthier than on the barn floor in the muddy blood. As she tiptoed to his bedside, he turned and opened his eyes. A smile bloomed on his face. And in a craggy voice, he said, "You must be the woman doctor."

Lillian shook her head. "Oh, gracious, that's Doctor Maddox—"

126

"I've met her. You're the young healer who's been taking care of my Edith." He nodded. "How can I ever repay you…?"

"Get well so you can care for her, that's all I ask." Lillian cleared her throat. "And stay away from that bull!"

Neil chuckled. "Harvey's normally fairly docile. Don't know what got into him."

"Thank heavens he didn't kill you and leave…"

Neil closed his eyes. "I thank the Lord every minute he didn't. My Edith has buried too many." He opened his eyes. "Toughest little gal I know."

"And I believe she will recover quite well."

Doctor Harris checked Neil's pulse. "Doctor Gardner, won't you check his heart with your stethoscope? You may find it sounds rather different from in the barn."

Lillian instinctively glanced around the room. "Mine is—"

Doctor Harris held out his. "Use mine, dear."

She took it, folded his blanket down, exposing his chest, and set the bell on his warm skin. She pressed her ear to the other end. The *whoosh, whoosh*, pumped steadily and rhythmically, making Lillian smile. She stood up and said, "A strong heart. Reckon it will beat for many years to come."

Just as Lillian was about to say her goodbyes, a man holding a young girl in his arms burst into the room. "Doc, she can hardly breathe!"

"Follow me," Doctor Harris said. "Lillian, you'll need to assist."

"I—I you sure?"

"Now, Doctor!"

Lillian followed them into another room and shut the door. She knew Doctor Maddox was in a rush to get going. "Let me go—"

"There's no time." Doctor Harris prodded the girl's neck. "Her lymph nodes are swollen, and she's burning a fever."

"She gonna live?" the man said, his eyes wide and asking.

Doctor Harris nodded as he examined the inside of her mouth. "Take a look."

"Excuse me," Lillian said to the sweat-coated man who was in dire need of a bath. She went to the side of the bed, bent over, and pressed a probe on the girl's tongue. "Her tonsils and pharynx are covered with whitish-gray spots."

Doctor Harris beamed. "That is correct! And if you look closely, the diphtheritic membrane is forming, causing her to struggle for air."

"The what?" The man's face paled.

Both doctors glanced at him. Then Doctor Harris said, "Her tonsils are infected and need to come out. Please wait outside. We'll fetch you after surgery."

"Surgery…?"

The man took a wobbly step.

Lillian grabbed him by the arm. "What's her name?"

"Jenny."

"And you're her father, I presume?"

"That's right."

Lillian escorted him into the hallway. "We'll fetch you when we're done. Don't fret, Mister…"

"Hughes. George Hughes."

Lillian propped him up against the wall. "It won't take long." She slipped back into the room. "Shall I fetch Doctor Maddox?"

"You'll do."

"But—"

"But nothing. You aspire to become a doctor, right?"

"Well, yes—but—"

"Come with me!" Doctor Harris carried Jenny into the surgical room and laid her on a table. She gasped for air, sounding as though she was being strangled.

"The chloroform's on the shelf."

Lillian plucked it off the ledge and poured a liberal amount onto a cloth. "Ready?"

"Go ahead." Doctor Harris talked in a confident tone.

Was he confident in Lillian or the procedure? She hoped for both. She held the cloth over Jenny's mouth and wiped a tear as it slid down the girl's cheek. "You'll be fine." Lillian smiled at her and stroked the brown ends of a pigtail.

He gestured to the wash table. "Clean up."

Lillian left the cloth on Jenny's nose, scrubbed her hands with antiseptic soap, and held her hands in the air, water dropping onto the plank floor. She was not sure what to do.

"We need to act quickly." Doctor Harris found a bottle of carbolic acid solution and a piece of cotton. "You want to swab?" He lifted a brow.

Lillian felt the color drain from her face. "I—uh…"

He thrust the cotton in her hand. "Get to work, Doctor." He turned and studied the girl's mouth."

Her hands shaking, Lillian wiped the solution over the lesions in Jenny's throat.

The gasping worsened.

"We need to insert a tube into the trachea so she can get air into her lungs."

"We?"

Doctor Harris shook his head. "I'll do it." He smiled at her.

Lillian sighed, willing her knees to stop knocking, angry at not being over the queasiness. How could she ever set up a practice feeling feeble at every turn of events?

"But I will need you to hold this syringe and draw saliva from Jenny's throat while I work on her neck."

Lillian felt weak and lightheaded. *God, don't let me faint!* The room began to spin. She closed her eyes and took in a deep breath.

"You with me, Doctor?"

She nodded, let out the breath slowly.

Doctor Harris braced Jenny's mouth open with a cloth pad, demonstrated how to keep her throat clear from saliva, and empty the syringe into a tin dish.

He laid his surgical instruments on a clean towel next to Jenny and picked up a knife with a long thin blade.

Lillian closed her eyes, wishing it was Doctor Maddox assisting the surgeon and not her. This confirmed being a doctor was not something she desired after all. She swallowed the bile burning her throat. *Lord, let me get through this.*

She opened her eyes and cleared saliva. Repeated the steps a couple of times before Jenny's breathing became stable.

"Why Doctor Gardner, you're the color of a lily pad."

Lilly Pad. It wasn't until she heard the doctor say those words that she realized how much she missed hearing her father's nickname.

"We'll let her rest now that she can breathe."

Lillian nodded as she sucked in oxygen. She found a chair, sank into it, and ducked her head between her legs. *Get me out of here!*

CHAPTER 21

"I thought I was going to retch all over the floor!" Lillian shook her head.

Doctor Maddox chuckled. "Be patient, *annwyl*, dear, this is much for your senses to take in. You have to get used to things. Use your head and not your heart."

"Not my heart? How can you say that? Our work is to save babies, fellas and ladies. You do not want me to care?"

"Now, now, I did not suggest for you to discount your empathy. We are in this line of work because we care. One has to learn to control emotions and work from the mind. You see, things like a well-oiled rifle can break down if not properly taken care of. It is all included in the circle of life. Death, disease, illness, we live in a damaged world, since the time Eve and Adam ate of the fruit. But there is comforting news."

Lillian grunted. "I don't see much light in the darkness."

"Oh, but there is." Doctor Maddox massaged her fingers. "God is always with us. Do you not read the good book?"

Lillian hung her head. "I do. Did. But it's at home."

"I can lend you mine." Doctor Maddox laughed. "But it is written in Welsh. I may have to translate it for you."

Lillian sighed. "God says He is with us, yes, but He does not always feel present."

"This is true. And I do not always understand His ways."

"Neither do I."

"Nevertheless, He promises He will be with us always. We must learn to trust Him, even when we do not feel His presence. All we can do is pray and leave a legacy of hope. God will do the rest of the work according to His will."

Hope. "I suppose." Lillian fingered her soiled skirt. "How long will we remain here?"

"Once I gather my supplies, we can pack our belongings and be on our way."

"Another adventure." Lillian's heart tugged at her to return home. Why did she feel so conflicted? She may never have the chance to experience a journey such as this. She prayed the Lord would give her a thankful heart and the endurance to finish what she started.

Lillian waved to Doctor Harris. He held up the pouches of herbs she had gifted him for treating her like a real doctor when most men frowned upon women physicians. "Come on now," she told the new bay packhorse Mali had named Owen, after her favorite uncle. She followed Doctor Maddox and Chwim toward the towering mountains. Her insides flip-flopped as she waved her heels on Asa's sides. She would miss young Edith.

The first few miles of the trip were an easy climb. Then they came into steep, rugged terrain, having to stop and let the horses rest.

"No wonder they gave Owen to me," Doctor Maddox said. "He may be on his last leg."

"I hope not. Maybe tomorrow he will be stronger." Lillian rubbed between his ears. His sides heaved and sweat coated his body, his chest foamy white. They had not gone that far, but looking back, Lillian realized how steep the terrain had been in the blistering heat. "Should we dismount and let them rest?"

"Heavens no. We have a ways to go before we make camp according to what Captain Miles told me." Doctor Maddox unrolled and studied the map. "Up ahead there is a stream. We'll let him drink and graze a spell. That may help."

"If not?"

"I'm sure there is something in those pouches of yours that will help a horse."

Lillian rummaged through the pouch carrying the herbs but found nothing that would help a horse. She rubbed his ears. "He's a sweet boy. I bet his previous owner depended on him. Even though his age slows him down, we are fortunate to have such a faithful partner with us." Mali agreed, taking sips of water and fanning her flushed face with a handful of leaves. When Owen's breathing slowed, they continued on at a slow but steady pace.

Lillian's thoughts ran wild. *How would they pack the supplies if Owen died? What would happen to the horse? Would they use the meat for food? Let the coyotes and mountain lions ravage the body?* She shivered, shaking her head and praying the animal would survive the trip.

The further up they climbed, the cooler the air became. Shade from pine, fir, and tamarack trees helped filter the sun. Lillian removed her Stetson and mopped her brow, allowing the mountain air to bathe her face and neck.

Hours later they reached the stream. Lush grass spiked along its pebbly banks. Lillian slid off her horse and led Asa and Owen to a spot clear enough to enter. Their heads dipped to the current. Lillian kneeled, scooped water into her cupped hands, and drank. Cool water slipped down her throat. She dipped her hat into the water, poured its contents on top of her head, and shrieked, startling the horses.

The water made her feel clean and refreshed, ready to tackle any hurdle that blocked their way. She led the horses to some grass and let them eat while Doctor Maddox watered Chwim. The sun hovered high in the sky, ready to make its descent.

"We can't linger." Doctor Maddox eyed the old bay. "Lighten his load. That may help." She looked up, seeming to examine the wind as it beat the tops of trees. She sniffed the air. "Move with haste!"

Lillian transferred some food the fort had donated to Lillian for assisting Doctor Harris, her first payment of any sort. It made her feel worthy and somewhat important. She couldn't remember a time she'd ever felt so valued. Yet this was not the time for such thinking.

Dirt, needles, and leaves pelted her face as she worked, the once calm breeze now howling through the forest. She knotted the packs a few times to make sure they held.

"Let's go!" Doctor Maddox hollered.

Lillian grabbed hold of Owen's lead rope, mounted Asa, and waved Mali forward. They traversed the rocky Indian trail until clouds of dirt blocked the way.

"We will have to spend the night here." Doctor Maddox hollered as she blocked her face from flailing debris. "It is too dangerous to continue on."

Lillian nodded several times. A boom thundered in the distance, startling Owen and causing him to pull back. "Whoa, boy." She hopped off Asa and settled the bony bay. Although their color was brown and black, she could easily tell the pair apart: Asa stood round and stocky; Owen sagged, his head drooping.

"Tie them to that tree." Doctor Maddox pointed a gnarled finger at a sturdy pine.

Lillian led them to the tree and looped the long reins around the trunk, low enough they could lie down. She started to knot them twice, then decided against it in case they needed to flee in a hurry. She unsaddled the horses, plopping each saddle under the cover of young fir trees. She wished they were close to a cave or rock overhang for added protection. But there were none in sight.

Once the horses were secure, the ladies found a spot under a couple of close fir trees with low branches. Lillian winced as another snap of thunder cracked the air. They laid out their bedding and picked at cold biscuits, dried fruit, and jerked beef.

Lillian yearned for the security of log walls and fresh vegetables. Was this the life of a doctor? Always traveling in extreme weather conditions, all hours of the day and night, little to no payment? Little sleep? How would Mali survive without her husband at her age?

Mali leaned against a tree trunk with her knees to her chest, slipped off her hat, and pulled a scarf over her head, her long nose peeking out. Lillian's chest thumped. She tried not to fret over her companion.

She pulled her Stetson low over her eyes and hugged her knees. Another crack shattered the heavens. They'd have to wait out the storm.

Lillian woke with a start. *She can't die!* She rubbed her eyes, replaying the nightmare in her mind. She saw Mali in a pine box, her face tinted gray. Turning toward where the healer had been perched, she was gone.

Her chest tight, Lillian sprang to her feet and cupped her hands around her mouth. "Doctor Maddox!" Glowing fingers of light scraped the sky. Seconds later, a crack made the hair on the back of her neck stand up. She shivered and called again, "Mali!"

Through the darkness, Lillian felt her way to the horses. One was gone. *Owen!* "Doctor Maddox, where are you?" Taking a step, she tripped over her skirt hem and toppled to the ground. Her eye slammed against a rock, causing her to yelp. "Ow!" She sprawled on the ground, a hand over her eye, and cried. Pain in her head throbbed. She groaned and rolled onto her knees. Blood stained her fingers, and the vision in her left eye blurred.

Tears stung her eyes. She pushed to her feet, followed the sound of the rushing creek, limping with slow, uneven steps, and washed her face. *Where is Mali?* As she sipped from her cupped hands, footsteps sounded behind her, and she jumped to her feet, whirling around. "There you are!"

"*Er mwyn y nefoedd*, for heaven's sake! What happened to your eye? It's as big as an egg!" Doctor Maddox waved her over. "Let me take a look at ya."

"I'm fine—"

"Come on, now. *Os gwelwch yn dda, annwyl*, please, dear." Doctor Maddox strode toward her.

"I'm coming. It's dark and rocky. No use in both of us bleedin'." Lillian picked her way back to the healer.

Cold hands touched her face. "It's too dark. Rip off the cuff of your shirtwaist and press the fabric against your eye. That will have to do for now."

Lillian did as suggested. "Owen's missing."

"I went looking for him—"

"Why would you do a fool thing like traipsing around in the middle of the night in a storm like this? Alone?" Lillian let out a sharp exhale. "Why didn't you wake me?" She winced from the pain of pressing on her injured eye too hard and moaned.

"I didn't go far…"

"Still?" Lillian chewed her lip, fighting back fresh tears. She refrained from sharing her frightful dream. "I can't do this without you."

Doctor Maddox patted Lillian's shoulder. "I am fine. Quit fretting, now. I had to try, he packs my medical supplies after all."

Strong winds whipped their hair loose.

Lillian nodded, brushing tendrils from her mouth and tucking them behind an ear, thankful it was August and not December with several feet of snow covering the ground in temperatures that turned fingers and toes black. She felt bad for scolding Mali and checked her tone. "What now?"

"Look!" Doctor Maddox pointed behind Lillian. The treetops glowed orange, hopping from tree to tree, racing toward them.

Lightning taking the form of tree roots jabbed the skyline, a crack so loud Lillian covered her ears and closed her eyes, her shoulders hunched over.

"*Cymer ofal,* look out!" Doctor Maddox pulled Lillian from the path of a falling pine. *Thwack!*

Lillian's breaths came fast as she clung to the healer, bits of bark and branches slapping her back and head. "Ow!" She walked Mali backward, farther from the fallen tree. Winds whipped their skirts. Horses cried out, rearing and sinking their haunches back until their lead ropes broke, setting them free. They spun and sprinted away. "Come back!" *Please, Lord!*

When the horses had gone about twenty feet, their faint forms circled, snorted, and stopped.

"I think we can catch them," Lillian said. "If you can see them, they're watching us."

"I cannot see them, but I trust you. Get them while I gather our belongings."

Lillian squinted in their direction. "You still there?" she whispered. She followed the downed tree to its busted off tip, wishing she had a candle large enough to illuminate the forest. "Whoa, babies," she crooned to them.

From the sounds of hooves on dried leaves, she knew they were stomping. "Stay there," she said, her voice a low lull. "I'm comin'…" With a hand out, she felt her way to the crackling debris. When the horses snorted, she stopped.

The broken lead ropes made her wish she'd paid more attention to the teachings of Spupaleena, Pekam, and Skumheist. She'd been foolish to think they were

140

only interested in teaching Hannah their ways. Thinking back, it was her who was withdrawn, causing them to think she had not been interested.

But she had been.

Still, she should have paid attention. She could have taken the time to learn to braid Indian hemp rope. She could have had spare ropes with her. *What now?*

A whinny sounded, bringing her out of her thoughts. Lillian took another step. Paused. Listened. When no crunching sounded she took more steps, talking to the horses in a soothing tone. Reassuring them they were safe. She held onto her skirt so it wouldn't rattle as much, her sleeves flopping against her arms. She could not afford to trip again.

Hooves stomped. She turned to a sky filled with yellow and orange scratches of light reaching for the heavens, singeing everything in their path. Crackles vibrated the woods. Smoke descended. Lillian coughed, covering her mouth and nose with her hand. She felt something trickle down the left side of her face, knowing her gash was still bleeding. She pressed an arm to her eye for several seconds before tearing the hem of her skirt and tying it over her nose and mouth.

A fit of coughing consumed her for a long moment. *The horses...* She held out a hand, the glow of the fire illuminating a path for her, and fumbled her way to them. Her fingers wrapped around Asa's short lead, allowing her to reach for Chwim. He backed up, wagging his head and showing the whites of his eyes.

"It's okay, boy." Lillian took another step. "I won't hurt you." When Chwim dropped his head, she caught him. She rushed to the tack and saddled and bridled the horses, loading as much of the medicine as she could and less food and other supplies.

Doctor Maddox took hold of Chwim and mounted. Asa pawed and squirmed, making it hard for Lillian to get on. "Easy, now…" Seconds later he stood long enough for her to get a foot into the stirrup. She sank into the saddle, her legs resting over twin packs Owen carried. It was awkward but had to be done. The people along the Pend Oreille needed the medications.

They headed east as ambers drifted down on them, the crackling deafening. Lillian felt the heat on her right side. *Protect us, Lord…*

As they climbed, a burning tree crashed, blocking the trail. "Let's go around—"

"How? There's no way," Doctor Maddox said. "It's too steep on either side."

"We can dip down—"

"No!" The healer frantically shook her head. "*Paid a bod yn hurt*, do not be daft!"

"There is no other path. Follow me!" Lillian reined Asa downhill. He picked his way over and between rocks, logs, and brush. Over her shoulder, the healer and her horse stood in the same spot. "Come on!" She waved them on. "Trust him."

The fire hovered over them, eating everything in its way.

Doctor Maddox glanced over her shoulder and kicked Chwim's sides. They too picked their way downhill and around the treetop. It smoldered, shooting willowy ringlets of smoke into the air. The tree's trunk and branches burned and popped, causing the already nervous horses to startle.

Lillian led them back up the hill and onto the trail. The saddlebags hanging over the saddle horn and under her legs rubbed her skin. She tried to reposition them but nothing helped, so she dug her heels into Asa's shoulder to keep from worsening the burn.

When Asa sped up, Lillian pulled on the reins to slow him down. He shook his head, prancing to the side. She let her legs dangle, praying her raw flesh wouldn't be so bad it bled.

CHAPTER 22

Dawn broke as they came down the mountain. Lillian could smell the smoke clinging to her clothing. Doctor Maddox looked haggard, her silver hair scraggly and loose around her shoulders. Lillian imagined she more than likely resembled a bear coming out of hibernation. She was thankful there was no looking glass to confirm her suspicions.

They went several miles until coming to the Pend Oreille River. It ran clear and inviting. The morning air felt stiff on her face. Her clothing stuck to her skin. "Shall we stop and clean up?"

Doctor Maddox gestured to a grassy spot next to the water. "Over there. I am famished."

"Me too." Lillian lifted her legs one at a time. Her skin stung, making her wince. She stopped near the river and again lifted her legs from the saddlebags. Tears stung her eyes. How would she get off and not make things worse? She placed a knee on the saddle and eased to the ground, gritting her teeth.

"You must be stiff from riding that way." Doctor Maddox stared at her from the saddle.

"I'm afraid my legs are raw."

"I have just what you need." The healer lugged herself out of the saddle, fished in her satchel, and pulled out a tin of salve. "Try a dab of this."

Lillian tugged off the lid and sniffed. "Smells like buck brush, alumroot, and plantain." She took another sniff. "Am I smelling sumac?"

Doctor Maddox smiled. "You are. I've been watching you…" She laughed. "Even old ladies like me can learn new ways. You have taught me much. And I am thankful for it."

I have taught her? Who would have thought? Lillian chortled, a spring in her step, and went to the river to bathe. When her skin was dry, she dabbed salve on the raw spots of the inside of her legs. She closed her eyes and sighed as the concoction soothed the burning. The healer was still in the river, so she started a fire and put on a pot of water for tea. "What would you like for breakfast?" she called to Mali.

"Anything…" Doctor Maddox sat in a shallow spot of the river, her arms circling the surface.

Lillian braided her curly locks and laid out dried fruit, hardtack, and nuts. She looked forward to getting settled and having a meal that stuck to her ribs. First thing she planned to make was cherry pudding. When the water was boiling, she dug out her dandelion leaves and plopped some into the kettle. "Come eat when you're ready."

Doctor Maddox pushed to her knees and rose, water dripping from her long hair, a bright smile pasted on her face. It was so warm out Lillian's dress was nearly dry. She rummaged in one of the saddlebags for a couple of tin plates and realized they were in the supplies that were left at the fire. And so were the cups.

"I, uh—oh, golly—our eating utensils are, well, back at the fire."

"That is a problem, at least for the tea. Our laps will do for the rations." Doctor Maddox tipped her head. "I think I have a solution." She padded to one of her packs and pulled out two small, tightly woven baskets. "Picked these up in Pinckney City."

Lillian turned the baskets over and examined the intricate designs. "They look like baskets made by the Sinyekst." She ran a finger over the cedar bark.

"The other afternoon when you were resting with Edith, I was summonsed to take a look at an Indian woman's son. I'm not sure where they are from. But she gave me the baskets for giving the *bachgen*, lad, a drop of medicine."

"What was wrong with him?"

"Nothing more than a toothache." She poured tea into a basket. "All he needed was a dab of clove oil rubbed on his tooth."

"What did you suggest his mother do for additional care?"

"Told her to see Doctor Harris. He's the one who gave it to me." The healer took a sip of tea. "He'll have to extract the tooth. It's rotten."

Lillian had no desire to learn that procedure. Her belly scrunched at the thought of it. She sipped her tea and took a bite of hardtack.

"How's your eye?" Doctor Maddox gestured to the purple lump surrounding Lillian's eye.

"I rubbed some of your salve on it. The pain is gone." Lillian fingered the skin with a tender touch. "I think the swelling is going down."

The healer nodded. "I can't recall what it looked like last night, but it does appear to be healing."

147

The ladies finished their meal and mounted. They traveled south. By the looks of Captain Miles' map, they would arrive at a large village by evening. Lillian swung a leg over the saddle horn and rode sidesaddle to give her skin a break from the saddlebags. Several miles downriver they stopped for a break. Heat radiated off the water. Lillian peeled off her Stetson and wiped her brow with the sleeve of her shirtwaist. After filling her body with cool water, she dabbed more salve on her legs and tied strips from her skirt over them for added comfort. The females and horses had a quick bite to eat and trudged on.

Lillian shifted in her saddle time and again, trying to find a more comfortable position. She was sure her legs would be bloody raw by the time they located the village. Along the way, they stopped several times for salve and for Mali to rest. Each time the healer closed her eyes and slept. Was she ill? Her chest rose and fell, rose and fell. Lillian let her sleep, wondering how old the woman was.

Pain relief from the last herbal slathering had worn off about the time lodge poles came into view. The village had to be around the next bend. Lillian bit her lip with each sway, holding in the urge to groan.

Sweat ran from Chwim's body, and Lillian was sure Asa was just as hot and exhausted. She wasn't sure she could make it without stopping. Wasn't sure Mali could make one more bend. There were not many settlers in these parts and no trading posts or hospitals. It was them and the River Paddlers. Did the men from Spupaleena's racing days live here? If so, would she be able to recognize them?

Doctor Maddox slumped in the saddle. Could she find a healer who could examine Mali?

When Lillian thought she couldn't tolerate one more of Asa's jarring steps, they rounded the bend to children playing with sticks and balls. Canoes floated downriver. Tule-mat lodges, like the ones in Spupaleena's village, lined the east bank of the Pend Oreille River. Men fished, women tended fires with sticks stacked with fish filets stuck in the dirt, leaning over low flames. The sounds and smells brought her back to the days of visiting the Sinyekst when she was a child.

Thinking back, those were some of her fondest childhood memories. Playing with the village children. Listening to Spupaleena and Hannah's horse banter. Trying to communicate without understanding but a few common words. Her mother had taught most of the children English while they had taught the Gardners much of the Salish language. It was always enough to get by.

It was Spupaleena and her family that learned to speak English. The others in the village relied on them to translate. The closer they got to the River Paddlers, the more Lillian realized they spoke a different language than Spupaleena's family. She would have to communicate with signs and gestures.

Lillian and Doctor Maddox rode through a shallow section of the river and rode into the heart of the village. Lillian dismounted. Women—both young and ripe— wearing cedar basket hats, twin braids, and abalone earrings stared at them, their expressions less than welcoming. A chill scampered down Lillian's back as several pointed at Mali's hat. She had heard most of the

Indians in the surrounding territories were peaceful, but they did not always welcome white settlers. She decided to prepare herself for the worst, something she'd heard Spupaleena's father, Skumheist, often say.

Hopefully they will not think we—two weary women—would try to take over their ways. Lillian smiled and waved at a woman about her age. The woman glanced at her companions, all surrounding their cook fire, and shook her head.

"Can you communicate with them?" Doctor Maddox's brows pinched.

Lillian shook her head. "They speak differently than what I was taught. So far, I have not recognized anything they've said.

The doctor eased from the saddle, her two small feet landing on the ground in a whisper. She adjusted her elongated hat, straightened her scarf, and dug her stethoscope from her satchel. "This may help." She held up the instrument with a smile and a twinkle in her eyes.

Lillian dug out various pouches of herbs—ones she'd seen as they rode downriver. "We need gifts. Put your stethoscope away or they will think it an offering."

"Ah, *le*. Fine idea." The doctor shuffled to her saddlebags.

Lillian picked out a few more pouches of herbs to share with them, ones she wasn't sure they were familiar with. She wished she had ribbon or cloth or some of her mama's wild berry preserves. She held up a pencil, then put it back, knowing they would have nothing to write with.

The dried herbs would have to do.

"Ready?" Doctor Maddox patted a parfleche bag. "I have needles, cloth, ribbon, knives. This shall do, huh?"

Lillian nodded. "Very much so." She followed the doctor around the village. Mali handed out gifts while Lillian tried to communicate with them. She showed them her various herbs. Some of the women shook their heads while others watched with knowing eyes. Only a few accepted samples of her medicinal plants.

When they'd gone around the village, Lillian gestured to a female elder with pleasing eyes the location they'd set up camp. With signs, she told them if anyone was injured or ill either one of the healers would be happy to help. They shook their heads, so she retrieved her stethoscope and showed them how it worked.

Pleasing Eyes frowned, shouting at them in their language. She pointed to their horses and shooed them away.

Doctor Maddox gasped. "Do they want my Chwim?" she whispered.

"I don't think so. I believe they are asking us to leave. And in not so polite a manner." Lillian smiled, nodded to the women, slipped her arm into Mali's, and headed for their horses. "Like when unknowns approach the Sinyekst, we will have to prove we are trustworthy."

"I understand," Doctor Maddox said, her expression filled with compassion. "We best set up camp."

Lillian helped the healer mount Chwim before she climbed into the saddle. They found a spot far enough from the village so as not to make the River Paddlers feel threatened, picketed their horses, and set up their tents. The Pend Oreille flowed lazily past their camp, causing a mixture of peace and homesickness to stir inside of her.

CHAPTER 23

August 15

Lillian continued to count the days by notching the strap of her pouch. Knife in hand, she was about to mark the day when two men in sturgeon-nosed bark canoes paddled past. Their narrowed eyes made her shiver. She prayed they would eventually accept her and Mali. She scored the buckskin strap then pulled out her journal and a new pen.

It has been a strenuous two days. I am exhausted and homesick. So much my heart aches. How will I tell Doctor Maddox that I feel it may be time for me to go home? I will have to find an appropriate escort as I cannot possibly travel back alone. I pray she will be safe on her own.

A pit formed in her belly as more men paddled past, all staring at her with frowns on their faces.

I also pray Pa and Mama will welcome me with open arms and not a switch for my backside. Perhaps I should remain a few more weeks and help Mali settle in. Make sure she is accepted. Or moves on. She is weary. A proud woman who would never admit to it. But I can see it in her eyes and in the way she shuffles about.

I suppose we will have to prove ourselves as Spupaleena and Hannah had by winning horse races against the River Paddlers she'd come into contact with. But by racing, I will not. There has to be another way. So far, I do not recognize any of the men. Then again, how would I? They all wear abalone earrings. I was too small to recall them. The stories Spupaleena and her family tell are all I know them by. If they still race, they may be in another territory. Or perhaps in Montana Territory hunting buffalo. What a sight that would be!

Lillian sighed, her chest constricted. She crossed her legs and tapped the pen on her journal.

The fire scared me enough to know home is where my heart is. Where I belong. While I have learned much on this journey, it is not one I want to take as a profession. I do not know what the Lord is calling me for, but trust in time He will make it clear.

For now, I will learn their language as best I can and try to assist Mali. We do work well together and I will miss her when we part.

Our food supply is dwindling. Having to leave the food and bring along the medical supplies was devastating. But again, I will have to trust my Creator. Koolenchooten as Spupaleena would say.

I sure hope Owen either made it out alive or died a swift death. How awful for the folks in Pinkney City to swindle Mali with a half-dead mount. It was truly a horrible act of brutality. He deserved better, as sweet as the ol' boy was.

As the sun's warm fingers massaged Lillian's tired muscles, her eyes grew heavy. She lay back in the grass, covered her face with her Stetson, and closed her eyes. She pondered ways to show the River Paddlers their sincerity. Birds sang in the distance. Horses snorted. The gentle swoosh of paddle to water lulled her.

Then came the ear-piercing shriek…

CHAPTER 24

Lillian sprang to her feet. Her hat, journal, and pencil flew to the ground. She swung around, searching for the scream. *Where was Doctor Maddox?*

A woman carrying an infant sprinted toward their camp. Lillian dashed to Mali's tent and found the healer asleep. She ducked inside and went to the woman's side. "Mali!" When the woman didn't move, Lillian shook her cold body. "Doctor Maddox, get up. We need you!"

Outside the tent, the woman's shrieks grew closer, her voice filling with terror. Knowing she needed to examine the doctor first, Lillian dug Mali's stethoscope out of her satchel and held the bell to the healer's chest, and the other end to her ear. She pressed the bell in different locations on Doctor Maddox's chest, hearing nothing.

"Wake up, Mali…" Her body trembled and tears blurred her vision. "No…" She had grown close to the old woman. They were companions. Friends. What was she supposed to do? She wasn't ready to be on her own. "You can't leave me!" Tears blurred her vision.

Stethoscope and satchel in hand, she dragged herself out of the tent and met the woman near the flap. "I can't—I'm sorry, but, my companion, she's—"

The woman shouted in her language, shoving a baby into Lillian's arm, tears streaming down her face.

A beefy man with abalone shell earrings joined the woman and held her arm, his eyes seeming to plead with her. She jerked away, shouting at him. "...*Alamiken*..."

Lillian recognized the name, knew it meant "Happy Man." She'd heard about their chief. Skumheist, Spupaleena's father, had talked about him at the wedding and had also referred to him as Chief Victor Alamiken. If only she could remember more of what he'd said. Had paid attention to the surrounding conversations.

The woman shook Lillian's shoulder, seeming to plead with her. Lillian laid the infant on a quilt with colorful patches in all shapes and directions. She pressed the bell of the stethoscope to the child's chest and listened. The heartbeat was rapid, and her lungs rattled in her tiny chest.

The man yelled at the woman, pointing to the instrument as if demons were coming out of it. Lillian held the infant, trying to ignore the couple. The baby's lips shone blue. She was not getting enough oxygen. *What now?*

She took a stick and pressed the infant's tongue down. There were no bumps like Jenny had in Doctor Harris's hospital. She needed him but knew the baby would not survive the trip.

Footfalls caught Lillian's attention. An older man with gray hair hovered over her, his lips pressed together. He talked in a stern voice to Chief Victor. He shook his head and shouted, pointing at Lillian. Her face heated. "*Help me...*"

The infant tipped her head back and went limp in Lillian's arms. "No…!" Lillian closed her eyes and prayed for wisdom. Begged God to tell her what to do. She squeezed her eyes shut. Then a high-pitched wail burst from the woman's mouth.

The sobbing woman fell to her knees, a hand on the infant's limp legs. She screamed and cried. Lillian felt tears stream down her face. "Why, God? Why?"

Lillian wiped her face. She wished she could stop crying. With no shovel, she didn't even know how to bury Mali. Her face ashen, the doctor lay on a trade blanket, the same kind Lillian's father used to get from Hudson's Bay Fort Colvile.

Her body trembled, and she felt woozy.

With what she assumed was the death of the chief's baby, she was afraid to ask for help. Afraid they'd take her life for not saving the infant—a beautiful baby with thick, soft hair the color of burned wood. A wide nose. Tiny brown fingers and toes. An otherwise healthy baby.

Then why had she died? She sniffed and wiped her nose with a neckerchief. An image of the child froze in her mind.

Was there something in her lungs? A crackle had shimmied down the stethoscope. Could she have had pneumonia? If so, the River Paddlers should have had the appropriate herbs to treat her. Had they sweat with her then dunked her in the cool water only to cause the illness? Would they blame her?

She shook her head and let the tears flow, wanting to ask Doctor Maddox how she handled her first death.

How she got through the pain. She'd probably tell her, *it takes time*. How much? Months? Years? Lillian stroked the woman's soft, silver hair, sobs escaping her lips. She pondered the idea of making a travois and taking Mali's body with her. She could wrap her friend in blankets. Chwim was plenty gentle and would do a fine job of transporting her to... Where would they go? She felt hopeless.

Lillian wiped her face and went in search of poles. When she returned, the body was gone. Lillian swallowed a scream and searched both tents, scrambling from one to the other, the riverbanks, and the woods surrounding the camp, coming up empty. *Where could she be?*

Bile burned her throat. Had the River Paddlers taken her body? But why? What would they do with it? She paced and muttered. How would she approach them without accusing them of theft? Would they burn the body, chanting away any bad medicine and evil spirits they thought she possessed? Would they then come after her?

Lillian doubled over and retched.

A deep groan escaped her lips as she wiped her mouth. Her body shook as if she were in freezing temperatures. She mopped her forehead and the back of her neck with a neckerchief. A hand pressed to her mouth, Lillian strode to the village and found Chief Victor.

"Where is she?" Lillian blinked several times, a sharp pain jabbing her chest.

He tipped his head.

"The doctor, where is she?" Lillian pointed a finger to their camp.

Chief Victor motioned for her to follow him. Lillian took shaky step after shaky step. Behind her, many

158

followed. She chewed the inside of her cheek, praying for her safety as they walked through the shadows of pine and fir trees. Wildflowers had long wilted and browned. Leaves crunched under her feet. She wet her lips, her salty saliva stinging them.

They stopped at two freshly dug graves—one for a baby and one for Mali. The bodies wrapped in trade blankets lay on cedar boughs inside their pits. A woman wearing Doctor Maddox's scarf hung around her neck came alongside Lillian. She gasped and ripped it from her neck, leaving a red burn mark. The woman screamed and took hold of the scarf, pulled. Lillian tugged harder. "Give it to me!"

Chief Victor shouted at the woman and she let go. Lillian clutched the wrap to her chest and fought back hot tears. "Why would you steal from a dead woman?"

The woman's gaze dropped. The chief gestured to both graves and began to talk in a calm tone, motioning to the sky, and back to the looming pit. Nothing made sense to Lillian. The baby's mother held a faceless doll to her chest as tears cascaded down her face. How could her baby have died? What had gone wrong?

Chief Victor went on for some time before motioning to a group of men to take their shovels and fill in the holes. One of the River Paddlers drummed and sang as the men worked. Lillian wept as dirt covered her companion's body. She felt alone—maybe even a little abandoned. Standing beside the grave, she thought about how far they'd come and lessons learned. Waves of sobs and numbness drifted in and out.

Once a fresh mound of dirt lay before her, Chief Victor turned and ambled away, the villagers following behind.

When Lillian was alone, she kneeled in the dirt and cried, realizing how wrong she was. They only had wanted to help. She would have to find the grieving woman and apologize. Offer her a gift. "What am I to do?"

She closed her eyes, prayed, and sang "Be Still My Soul." It was dark when she stood, said her final farewell, and made her way back to camp. Mindlessly, she watered the horses and staked them out. Chwim whinnied as she walked away as though asking for his companion.

Lillian took in a deep breath. Her tummy growled. The thought of food made her queasy. After sipping a handful of water, she went to bed. Sorrowful wales drifted through the valley. Her heavy eyes closed. She curled into a ball, wishing Doctor Maddox was alive and sleeping in the tent next to hers.

Bright light and heat pulsed throughout Lillian's tent. One of the horses snorted. Hoof steps shuffled outside. She sat up and rubbed her eyes, wincing at the still tender one. She fingered the slightly puffy tissue on the left side of her face, found the tin of salve, and dabbed a tad of it onto the swollen area.

Her full bladder called for her to rise and empty its contents. She ducked out of the tent to baskets of native vegetables including camas, dried salmon, and a bladder of water, all laid on a—Lillian blinked several times— quilt. Was she seeing things? She stooped and fingered the blocks of flour and sugar sack squares stitched with obvious deft fingers. Where had they gotten the quilt from?

Lillian stood and studied the village. The woman who had Mali's scarf scowled at her from the river's edge. "Wait!"

The woman shook her head and rushed off. Lillian grunted and went in search of a suitable shrub to do her morning business. When done, she strode to the river, swirled a neckerchief in the cool water, and washed her face and neck. She sat in the warm sand and allowed a few tears to flow. *Why did Mali have to die?*

After watching a few men fish with cone-shaped weirs, she rose, fetched her journal, and settled in a grassy patch on the bank.

Chapter 25

August 16

I miss her. Plain and simple. She was like a grandmother to me. May God rest her soul. Mali will be pleased to be buried among the River Paddlers. She loved them even though she felt rejected. She believed in them. More than I did, as ashamed as I am.

Fear has consumed me as I have no knowledge of how I will get home with no escort. It is not the Indians I'm afraid of, but the men who love their liquor. The stories Pa has told Mama churn my stomach. But I cannot remain here.

I suppose I will have to eat some of the bounty the villagers have gifted to me, pack, and find my way back home. I was surprised to wake and find baskets of their food. They confuse me. I feel they have blamed me for the death of the infant. But why then would they bury Doctor Maddox and give me food? If I wasn't so tired, I could probably think clearly.

She shook her head.

It makes me wonder if by helping me they hope I will soon leave. If only I had the strength to pack. The will to travel alone. The courage to leave.

Lillian sniffed.

She turned the page in her journal and sketched the village, the River Paddlers in their bark canoes, the infant in her mother's arms, Doctor Maddox and her tall hat and white scarf, the baskets of food on the crazy quilt, salmon on tall sticks pitched over a smoldering fire, the graves. She turned another page and in large letters penned:

We must always leave a legacy of hope.

CHAPTER 26

Lillian tightened the last of the latigo strings securing the saddlebags on Chwim and mounted Asa. She gripped Chwim's lead rope and headed toward the shallow crossing. She stopped so the horses could get a drink. It would be a while before they stopped to rest. Children playing near the water watched them with wide eyes. One little girl waved, a small smile on her face.

A part of Lillian felt sad. She looked forward to working with the River Paddlers and learning their ways as she'd learned the Sinyekst's. The grave was not visible through the trees, but she still squinted at it. "It has been a pleasure and honor serving with you, *annwyl*, dear Mali."

Asa stepped onto a sandy beach and climbed a small bank, Chwim willingly following behind. A woman shouting echoed behind Lillian. She reined Asa to a halt and turned him around. The woman waved at her. Was she beckoning her to come back? Lillian tipped her Stetson back and squinted. She waved her legs on Asa's sides and went to find out what the woman wanted.

When on the other side, Lillian dismounted by the woman with prominent cheekbones, tight twin braids, abalone earrings, and a round face. She had a soft glow about her. Lillian found the woman's name to be Yellow Owl, and she wanted Lillian to stay and not let the chief and his wife's grief cause her to leave. Yellow Owl signed about visions she had of a doctor coming with medicines that could and would help her people. Lillian thought about the medicines in Mali's satchel. She was not familiar with all of them but had noticed various uses printed on the glass bottles. The woman looked desperate. But why? They had a healer in the village. Why her?

Lillian agreed to stay and went back to the site she and Mali had camped. After pitching her tent and setting up the other one for a make-shift clinic, she found Yellow Owl and told her she was ready to see patients. On her way back, she prayed God would guide her. She'd never felt so uncertain in all her life.

But after several hours no one had come for her services. Was it because she was a woman? Perhaps still a child through their eyes?

Late afternoon and after showing Yellow Owl the herbs she had in stock, the two women paddled downriver in a canoe in search of additional plants to dig and dry. Lillian marveled at the craftsmanship of the cedar-framed canoe with a western white pine bark covering. Ponderosa pines and cottonwood trees reflected in the water as the canoe glided across its surface. High mountains filled with trees rose on either side of the river, a prosperous valley anchoring them down. Geese honked as they flew overhead. Ducks and other fowl dove for fish.

For a moment all of her worries faded.

The greens, white, yellow, and brown in the water allowed Lillian's mind to drift to a place she felt at peace with the world. She had always looked forward to being on the water with Spupaleena's family. Loved fishing.

Loved the calm feeling when in a canoe on a breezeless day.

A ways downriver, they pulled the canoe onto shore, grabbed digging sticks made of hardwood and deer antler, buckskin pouches, and baskets. Lillian stepped out of the canoe and examined a patch of wetland plants. Their soft green leaves were shaped like arrows and rose from the water. Yellow Owl joined her and with her hands told how ducks, other waterfowl, and songbirds feasted on the seeds while muskrat, beaver, and porcupine loved the tubers. She told a story of when her family stole the potatoes from muskrat nests when times were hard.

Lillian reached for a plant, but Yellow Owl stopped her, shaking her head, gesturing their harvest would be in the season of when darkness approaches, or what Lillian knew as October. Delicate white flowers threaded through leaves towered over them.

Yellow Owl took Lillian to a place she could collect several plants—ones she already had and ones new to her. They collected and conversed with words and gestures as they came across various mushrooms on the ground and attached to trees. Yellow Owl taught her which ones were edible and which ones to avoid.

Lillian found a friend in Yellow Owl, guessing they were near the same age. How grand it would be for her and maybe a relative to escort her home.

Together, they gathered red willow bark, husk husk, chocolate tips, black and blue camas, and rattlesnake plantain. When done, they returned to the village, and Lillian packed her harvest into the clinic. She hummed as she laid them out to dry on a blanket. In the distance, sounds of drumming and rattles, chanting, and something like sticks beating wood caught her attention.

Because dusk threatened daylight, she hurried to finish her task, ate food from the gifted baskets left for her that morning, and made her way to groups of men gathered outside the tule-mat lodges, playing a game with sticks and bones. Women helped beat on hand drums and sing while the men played the game, chanted, and drummed.

Yellow Owl met her and explained that the River Paddlers were playing a game called Stick and Bone Game to brighten the mood after the infant's death and burial. She encouraged Lillian to get to know the game and take time to enjoy herself after her companion's death.

Yellow Owl explained the game: two opposing teams of three or five sit in a line and face one another and use twelve long painted sticks stuck into the ground to keep score. Lillian and Yellow Owl happened to take a seat on the south end of the split crowd. At the start of the game, men played for a single stick called the kick stick, and the winner chose if they want the additional stick or not—making a total of six instead of five sticks for scoring. Those not hiding or guessing where the bones were, beat sticks against a pole laid on the ground at their feet as they sang and chanted during the game.

Already voices were deafening. As Lillian watched, she recalled Skumheist having played the game a time or two but had not paid attention to the rules.

Two players on the other side of her hid two white bones and two bones with black marks carved in the middle in their hands, fists up so all could see. Lillian had a hard time keeping track of it all. She leaned closer as one player who sat on her side, opposite of the two players hiding bones, tried to guess which hand the white bones were in.

Lillian assumed the guesser was using quick hand movements, facial gestures, chanting, cheers, and rattles to try to intimidate their rivals. Yellow Owl held up a black bone and shook her head, gestured if the black-marked bones are guessed, the team receives one to two of eleven sticks depending if they get one or both guesses correct. Yellow Owl held up a white bone and nodded, a wide smile on her face. If they guess the white bones, they get the bones and keep playing. Lillian decided the white bones were what players coveted and needed to win.

In the end, whoever had won all eleven sticks, Yellow Owl signaled, wins. Winning teams take their opponents' most prized possessions: horses, spears, knives, weirs, jewelry, blankets—anything they valued and brought to barter.

Yellow Owl slouched. Women were only allowed to sing and cheer. She patted the seat next to her and shrugged.

Lillian was eager to try to guess the white bones, if only in her head. Anything to push the sorrow in her heart away.

A few women stared at her and scowled. Most ignored her. At a point when she felt comfortable, she sang and chanted and cheered. Sometimes she guessed correctly, and other times she guessed the marked bones. But it didn't matter because for the first time in weeks, she laughed.

Yellow Owl was right, the festive game made her feel better. It even made her feel like she was a part of their community.

Sometime during the Stick Games, Chief Victor came and sat by Lillian. "Are you enjoying the game?" He smiled at her, his gray shoulder-length hair parted on the side. A neckerchief was tied around his neck.

"You speak English?"

He chuckled. "Father DeSmet baptized and taught many of us your ways."

Lillian shook her head. "Oh, but I'm not Catholic." She could barely hear him over the pounding of drums and loud voices.

"Yet we honor the same Creator."

"Yes, we do." Lillian smiled at him. He made her feel welcome. A man of great peace.

"The baby's death, it is not your fault." Chief Victor gave her a basket of dried venison. "Take this and know we do not blame you."

Lillian took the basket and bit her lip, stopping tears from blurring her vision. "Thank you. I accept this gift with a grateful heart."

Chief Victor nodded and handed her a neckerchief. "It is good to laugh and not mourn. I am sorry for your doctor companion. Know you may remain here as long as you need."

Lillian dabbed her eyes and nodded.

It was late into the evening when she yawned, said good night to Yellow Owl, and went to bed. She wanted to write in her journal but couldn't seem to light the lantern in the dark, so she laid on her bedroll and let the drumming and chanting lull her to sleep.

It was still dark outside when Yellow Owl woke up Lillian. "What is it?" The woman tugged on Lillian's shirtsleeve and rambled on in her native tongue. Lillian

170

rose and followed her to the river. A thin layer of smoke from the forest fire hovered over the water. They got in a canoe and paddled to the middle of a wide section of the Pend Oreille.

In a canoe lay a young woman, her abdomen extended with child. She panted and cried out, cradling her enlarged belly. "What is she doing out here in the middle of the night?" Light from a full moon skated across the river.

Yellow Owl blinked several times and stared at Lillian. She shook her head.

"Who in their right mind would give birth in the middle of a river?" Lillian prayed she would not tip the canoe over as she put one foot into the woman's boat and crawled in. "This is foolish!" She checked the woman and prepared for birth, knowing the baby would come at any minute.

Lillian prayed there would be no complications, like when Sadie gave birth to Henry. The woman pushed, biting down on a stick. Lillian tried to position herself so the canoe would not rock too hard. Yellow Owl held both boats together. The woman pushed a few more times before a baby boy emerged.

Lillian glanced around for a blanket and there was none. She clutched the infant close to her chest to keep him warm. Yellow Owl tapped her shoulder and held out a buckskin hide. Lillian placed the baby in the preserved deerskin and let her friend tend to the boy while she cared for the young mother.

"Let's get back to camp," Lillian said. "She's exhausted."

Once mother and child were secure, Lillian paddled to shore and pulled the canoe's tip onto the sand. Yellow

Owl kept the baby in her canoe while she helped Lillian get the mother onto dry land.

"I'll take her to the clinic." Lillian pointed to the tent. Yellow Owl nodded and fetched the infant. The clinic bed was still full of wilted plants, so Lillian moved mother and child to her bedroll. She settled them in, found a blanket, and bedded down under the stars. Yellow Owl hugged Lillian, signed her appreciation, and laid down on a buffalo hide beside her.

Lillian closed her eyes. *Thank you, Lord, for your guidance.* Yellow Owl's friendship and trust ignited Lillian's faith as a healer. She took in a deep breath and pushed out any remaining doubt.

CHAPTER 27

August 17

Lillian's journal rested on her lap as she leaned against an aspen. She inhaled the smoky morning air. The newborn had woken a few times during the night, and his mother seemed to handle his care as though he were the sixth in line.

Never did I dream I would deliver a baby in a canoe! Thankfully mother and child are safe, tucked under a blanket in my tent. I was so terribly tired when I caught the boy, I greeted him with blurred vision. Thankfully, he landed in my hands and did not slip into the cold river. What a tragedy that would have been. Surely the villagers would have chased me out if anything bad had happened.

I might go as far as saying Providence caught him for me.

And what a bundle of joy. Dark hair as thick as prairie grass. Round eyes. Dark skin. And boy, was he chubby. Holding him felt right.

Just when I thought I'd been rejected, it seems I have found a strong bond with Yellow Owl. She is a delightful young woman. Her face is as soft and gentle as the delicate petals of the purple shooting star wildflowers we have been admiring in the area. I still do not understand why she has taken a liking to me. Nevertheless, I'm happy she has.

Chief Victor is a gentle soul. It pleases me to know he can speak English. We will be able to communicate more effectively. I believe more of the River Paddlers speak it as well and are hiding it from me. I will not be surprised if Yellow Owl knows the language.

I am happy here and will remain a day or two before I travel home. I miss mama more than she will ever know. How can I show her how sorry I am? I pray the Lord will give me divine words when we greet one another. I pray she will forgive me. Papa too. I am in no hurry to see Delbert. I'm sure he will have plenty to say to me. None of it heartwarming.

There are a few settlers in the area. Tomorrow I shall call on them and see if they need any medical attention. I can always leave them with herbs and knowledge about how to harvest, make poultices, and consume them.

Today is the first time I feel like a real healer—Doctor Gardner.

Lillian yawned and closed her eyes. Birds sang, the sounds of horses snorting and milling about filled her ears. Love filled her heart.

CHAPTER 28

Lillian felt sweat scuttle down her back. One at a time, she opened her eyes, blocking the hazy sun with a hand. She found her hat on the ground, dusted off a thin layer of ash, and settled it on her head, pulling the brim low. Her lips hurt, so she ran her tongue over them, feeling the cracks in her flesh.

She pushed to her feet and stretched her sore back. *The baby.* She rushed to her tent only to find it empty, figuring mother and child went to their lodge. Still, her heart sank. She hoped to examine the baby one last time before they went home.

While in the shelter, she slipped into a green gingham dress, braided her hair, and patted her brown Stetson on her head. Peaking from a bag was Mali's tall hat. She pulled it out, blew the dust and ash off it, ran a finger over the soft brim, and dabbed her eyes with a neckerchief. She wondered if she should keep it. If it would survive the trip home. Perhaps Yellow Owl would like to have it. She set it down and tied the neckerchief around her neck.

After a meager meal of dried fish and fruit, cold camas cakes, and rosehip tea, she gathered a selection of herbs to share with the settlers, Mali's satchel, and saddled Asa. "Sorry, Chwim, but you'll have to stay here and look after things." She scratched his neck and kissed his nose. She led Chwim to the river and let him drink before securing him tightly to a tree. She double-checked her knots to make sure he would not escape and follow them.

Losing Owen tugged on her heartstrings. One dead horse was too many.

She mounted Asa and headed for the river. She let her bay drink before urging him forward, took off her neckerchief, swirled it in the river, and tied it back on. She coughed, knowing the smoke from the forest fire would soon clog her lungs. The baby came to mind. Hopefully, the parents would have a cloth to cover his mouth with. She prayed for rain to drench the flames and clear the air.

The first settlement was several miles south. She looked forward to discovering new territory and if she stumbled on plants to harvest, all the better.

The first cabin she came upon was at the base of a hill. The closer she got, she realized it was not finished. As she approached, she hollered, "Hello to the cabin…" With no answer, she rode around the perimeter of the place. The area was littered with log ends and wood shavings, handsaws, an ax, and other tools. "Good morning, I'm Doctor Gardner, is anyone home?" she hollered.

Lillian rounded a corner to a small corral and covering for one or two animals. Someone had set up a lean-to under a tall fir tree. Near the camp was a fire pit; Dutch oven; and an assortment of tin cookware and utensils; a pan with leftover beans, cup, a plate with bean juice stuck to it, fork and spoon, and a coffee pot.

Lillian dismounted and held a hand over the fire. Light heat radiated from white coals. Lifting the lid from the coffee pot revealed it was half-empty. "Hmm." She scanned the area, squinted her eyes. "Is that…?" She took a few steps before lifting her skirt and tearing uphill. She stopped at the head of a young unconscious man with the lower part of his legs caught under a thick pine. She assumed a horse had been attached to the log, spooked, and ran off. *What on earth had startled the animal?*

The hair on the back of her neck rose. She scanned the woods but saw nothing to alarm her.

"Can you hear me?" Lillian kneeled and pressed a hand to his shoulder. She stood and with a grunt tried to lift the log, but it was too heavy. "Oh, Lord, how am I going to get this log off his leg?" The man's horse was not in sight.

Blood stained black curls around his right ear. She fingered the deep cut, realizing she needed the satchel. Doctor Maddox's instructions of tending to the most severe injuries first sprang into her mind, so she focused on his leg first. "I need to get this log off your leg if you can hear me. Then I'll tend to your wounds."

She hurried to Asa, fetched needed supplies, broke sturdy branches, and peeled bark from trees. A few steps uphill and she turned around, untied Asa, and rummaged around until she found a hunk of rope. She prayed as she led her gelding to the twiggy man, sure his leg was broken. He was too thin to withstand such an injury.

"My name's Doctor Lillian Gardner and I'm going to fix you up…" She sat back on her heels and sighed. "I'm gonna have to get that log off your leg."

She looped one end of the rope around the log and dallied the other end to the saddle horn. *How am I going to lift this up and not drag it over his leg?* She assessed the situation, prayed, and asked Asa to back, keeping one hand on the reins and one on the rope near the log.

The man cried out, startling both Asa and Lillian. The bay jerked back, swinging the log to the side and off his leg. As the wood rolled over, it struck Lillian. "Ouch!" Tears burned her eyes as she grasped her leg. The reins dropped and Asa backed, tightening the rope.

"Whoa!" she hollered. "Stop!" Asa kept going, taking the log with him. She lunged at the rein and grabbed hold. The bay halted and took a step forward, leaving enough slack in the rope she could unwind it from the saddle horn.

Lillian dropped the rope and hobbled to the man's side. Even though he had screamed, he was still out cold. *Thank goodness!* She pulled up her skirt, exposing her bloody shin and torn stocking. She peeled the wet undergarment off her leg, wiped it with a scrap of flannel, and dabbed salve on the gash. She moved to the man.

His trouser leg was torn, exposing a red, swollen area about six inches below the knee. His fingers wiggled, reaching for his thigh. "I think your leg is broken, mister. Can you tell me if anything else hurts?" He shook his head, his eyes squeezed shut.

"Oh dear, I must take a look. Forgive me for…" She turned her head, her tummy woozy, not wanting to cause him further agony. Since the log had been across his tibia, she figured that had to be the only place with a break. She drew her knife from her boot and cut his pant leg off from the thigh down, which exposed another swollen area. "Oh, dear. Did the log hit here"—she gently touched the side of his thigh—"before it landed on your shin?" He nodded.

"Gracious! You're a mess," Lillian said with a smile. "This is gonna hurt." She gave him some red willow bark

178

for pain, stuck a stick in his mouth, set her foot in his armpit, and tugged on his knee, trying to set the femur first. She jerked when he screamed. *I can do this...*

"Hold on, I have another one..." She wrapped his thigh and prayed, not knowing what pulling on his ankle would do to his cracked femur. She didn't know what else to do. *Help me, Lord.* She grabbed his ankle with both hands and pulled. When he screamed, she chewed on her bottom lip, keeping hold of the ankle until she felt the bones align and the lumps disappeared, then slowly released her grip.

The man was again unconscious. "No wonder you didn't holler," Lillian sighed. "Just as well." She sat on her heels for a moment and let her head settle. Once the spinning stopped and the queasiness eased, she placed sticks and bark on either side of the broken bones to stabilize them and wound a rope around the length of his leg.

Next, she fished in the satchel and found boric acid, uncorked the bottle, took a sniff, winced, and stuffed the cork back in. Plunging back into the satchel, she pulled out a needle and thread and stitched the gash behind his ear, sewing layers of muscle and skin together until the wound was closed. Satisfied with her work, she untied her pouch from the saddle and found rattlesnake plantain, made a poultice with a leaf, added salve to make the herbs stick and pressed it on the wound. "That will have to do for now, mister."

Asa grazed nearby. She studied the man's etched face. "How am I going to get you to your camp?" Why was he in the wilderness alone? Did he have a family? If so, where were they? He appeared to be of marrying age. "Hmmm." She went back to where he had been sawing logs and found his ax, chopped down two young aspen

179

trees, and built a travois. She gathered a couple of blankets and padded the poles, and dragged him onto the sledge. After attaching Asa to the two long poles, she began the slow descent to his tent, thankful it was a short one-hundred yards.

When they came to the man's camp, Lillian dismounted and unhitched the travois. Her arms shaky and fatigued, she plopped the poles of the travois on the ground harder than intended. "Oh my..." The man groaned, and Lillian gasped. "Forgive me, mister..." She wished she knew his name.

His eyes rolled around as though trying to open. She hovered over him, holding a breath. Then let it out when he settled, his eyes closed. Grabbing hold of the blanket corners, she tugged him into the tent, wiped her brow with her neckerchief, and found water. She gulped from her canteen—from the canteen Mali had used—and held it close. She needed the doctor's wisdom and experience.

Shaking her head, Lillian looped the strap of the canteen over the saddle horn and tied Asa to a tree. Her tummy groaned. She fished through her saddlebag and chewed on dried salmon and camas cakes, yearning for her mother's fried cabbage and onions and fresh venison. Or beef. Anything straight from the garden. And apple pie.

She didn't know what to do. Who to fetch for help. Where was the nearest hospital? With the pass closed, she feared there'd be no way to Fort Colville.

A deep pit formed in her belly, making it hard to swallow her food. She sighed, took a swig of water. The only thing she could do was to ride back to the River Paddler's village and fetch their healer.

She dug out morphine and laudanum from Doctor Maddox's satchel, choosing the morphine and administering the proper dosage, and said a quick prayer, hoping the man's horse was safe and would wander back to camp. She checked his splint, making sure it was secure, and ducked out of the lean-to.

Asa stood quietly in the shade of the tree he was tied to, his eyes half-mast. She stroked his neck and untied him. After a long drink of water, she mounted and kicked her bay into a fast trot.

Lillian found Yellow Owl weaving a basket in the shade of pine trees. Strips of bark and dyed grass lay on a trade blanket. Lillian jumped off Asa and said, "I need your healer." She gestured her need for help from the medicine man as she spoke. Yellow Owl tipped her head. Lillian repeated the words and hand motions.

Yellow Owl nodded and pointed to a lodge with two young boys pretending to spear imaginary fish with sticks near its flap door. Lillian nodded and rushed to the lodge. She stopped, not knowing how to announce herself. After a long moment, she cleared her throat. "Hello to the lodge. I need help," she said in a rather loud voice. "May I enter?" When no one appeared, she shook the flap door.

The boys stopped playing, their jaws slack and eyes round. She again cleared her throat and clapped her hands. "I'm coming in…" She ducked inside and let her eyes adjust to the darkness.

On a buffalo robe lay a man with wisps of gray interlaced with black hair. A knife handle stuck out of his right leg. His body quaked, his eyes wide. A young man beside him stood, shouting and pointing to the flap door.

She figured the boy was telling her to get out. Instead, she kneeled beside the wounded man.

The medicine man began to chant. Without thinking, Lillian pulled out the blade, examined inside the gash, and pressed a hand to the wound. The young man screamed at her, jabbing a finger in her face. She took one of the medicine man's hands and pressed it to the wound, retrieved the satchel, pulled out a needle and thread, and stitched the cut, layer by layer.

"He's going to be fine," Lillian said. She prayed for the man as she stitched, knowing the size of the gash would take a while to sew but was not life-threatening. After the thread was snipped, she placed herbs and salve on a leaf and pressed it against the wound.

She gestured for the medicine man to follow her. "A man is dying!" She tugged at his arm. He jerked away and pushed her to the ground. She sprang to her feet and yelled, "You need to follow me. He will die if you don't help him!" She jabbed a finger at his chest, then swung it over to the lodge flap. He stepped back, eyes wide. She waved for him to come, pleading.

He glanced at the young man who shook his head, his upper lip curled. The healer grunted and ducked out of the lodge. He found a horse and hopped on, staring at Lillian. She mounted Asa and tore off. Lillian prayed the man she'd found was still alive.

Chapter 29

When Lillian and the healer arrived at the man's camp, Lillian found her stethoscope and checked his heart rate. A faint swoosh came through the wooden instrument. His breaths were shallow but steady. She sighed, relieved he was still alive. Next, she checked his lungs. There was a slight gurgle to them. She made a note to give him something to prevent pneumonia.

The healer stared at her as though she was some kind of monster. She passed the instrument to him and let him listen. With her guidance, he pressed the bell to the man's chest and put his ear to the other end and listened. He threw the stethoscope and shouted at her, his eyes wide.

Lillian didn't understand if he was mad or frightened. Then he made the sign for evil spirits. She shook her head. "This is a tool to help diagnose and heal," she said as if he could understand her. How could she convince him her stethoscope was not harmful or bad medicine? She pointed to the injured man and gestured for them to take him back to the village.

The healer shook his head. She retrieved her stethoscope and listened again, realizing she should have brought the chief to translate. She tipped her head.

"There are many in your village who speak English. I have a feeling you can understand me. Am I right?"

The healer pursed his lips.

"We need to get him back to the village. He can't stay here by himself and—"

He motioned for her to remain with the man. She shook her head. "I cannot lift him. I need your help. He's too tall." He nodded.

Nearby, brush rattled. Lillian stood and stepped from the lean-to. A brown giant of a horse appeared from the trees. She held still, not wanting to spook the animal. Blood dribbled from a gash on his shoulder. He stopped, his gaze on her. She glanced away, her head angled downward. She'd never seen a horse that huge before. He dropped his head, but it sprang up when she took a step toward him.

"Whoa, boy. Come on, now," Lillian said, her tone soothing. "I won't hurt you." Her gaze on the ground, she held out a hand and crept toward him. He snorted and backed his massive hooves up. As did she, scrunching her toes inside her boots. She could imagine the kind of damage he would do by stepping on her feet. What could she offer him to draw him in? While looking for something, anything that would do, she came across a woman's hair ribbon. "He does have a wife." She needed to make sure he lived.

She spun around to find the healer with the brown horse towering over them, its lead rope in hand. "Oh! You caught him." Her face heated. She never did have a connection with horses like Hannah had.

He handed her the rope. "Here."

"Here?" Lillian shook her head. "So, you do speak English." She pressed a hand on her hip.

"Only when I want to."

184

Lillian slipped the ribbon in her skirt pocket and took the lead. "Suppose we need to get the travois attached to this one." She reached to stroke his nose, admiring the white blaze on his face, and he startled, pulling Lillian off balance. The healer caught her and propped her on her feet. He scowled, grunted, and strode to the lean-to.

Lillian checked the horse over, tended to his wounds, and fetched the sledge. The closer it got to the horse, he backed up, his round eyes on the monster. "All right..." She looked him over. "For now I'm going to call you— Shorty." She laughed. "It's that or Tenderfoot." He snorted. She clutched the lead rope and pulled on one of the poles of the travois. Shorty pulled the rope out of her hands and trotted away. "Ouch!" Tears burned her eyes as she shook her hand.

The healer laughed from the shade of a pine tree. Lillian groaned. "Are you going to help me?" He shook his head. "You either do not like me as a woman or a female healer, no matter which one, this man needs medical attention."

"You do not need me."

"As you can see, I'm not strong enough to do this alone. With the two of us, we can hook up the travois."

"You are stronger than you think. You have lost faith in yourself as a healer."

"If that were true, I would not be here trying to save this fella's life."

He sat stoned faced.

She grunted, found a jar of salve, rubbed a glob on the rope burns, and wound flannel around her hands. She watched the brown horse graze. "What would Hannah do?"

When tending the garden, Lillian had secretly watched her sister work with young horses. Hannah would toss sugar sacks and blankets over their backs and against their legs to help calm them. Lillian searched for and found an empty sugar sack. On the first attempt, she smacked the sack too hard against Shorty's leg and he leaped like a frog, spun around as fast as a giant animal could, and kicked the air, his heavy frame leaving puffs of dirt when his plate-sized hooves hit the ground.

Lillian shuffled backward, ran into the log, and fell, hitting her head. A scream rushed from her mouth and she lay in the dirt for a spell, her eyes squeezed shut. She flung an arm over her eyes, expecting the healer to come running and fret over her.

But he didn't.

When her head stopped spinning she sat up, gave her head a couple of slow shakes, coughed. Groaned. Squeezed her eyes shut. The healer looked as though he was sleeping. A rattled snore confirmed her suspicions. Lillian had an urge to rush over and kick his shins.

But she didn't.

"Humph." After brushing dirt and wood chips off her clothing, Lillian marched over to Shorty and reached for the lead rope. He trotted away a few yards, turned, and stared at her. "Are you daring me?"

Behind her, a subtle snicker came from the healer's direction. She spun around to his closed eyes, huffed, and approached the horse like she'd seen her sister hook a hard-to-catch colt. Her gaze on Shorty's shoulders, she held out a hand so he could snag her scent. She stepped to the side, arching toward his hindquarters. One of his hind feet moved, then another foot shuffled, making his hip swing to the side as he faced Lillian.

Within a few steps, Lillian was close enough to take hold of the lead rope. "Good boy." She dragged out "boy" and rubbed his neck, wishing she had a carrot to feed him. Footsteps caught her attention. She twisted around to find the healer stalking away. "Where are you going?"

He held up a hand and waved. She picked up her skirts and hurried to him. "I need your help."

"You are slow," he said. "Besides, you know what you are doing."

"You can see the horse has been frightened."

"Standing Bear needs me."

"The man with the knife stuck in his leg?"

The healer kept walking.

"Standing Bear is fine. This man is struggling to live." Lillian clutched his arm and pulled him around. He shoved her hand away, his eyes narrow. "Please, help us."

"If you want to be a healer, you must do this on your own." For a short moment his gaze locked on her, and then he left.

Lillian groaned. "How am I going to get him on the travois?" She went back to the lean-to to check on her patient. His eyes were open as he looked around, his gaze landing on her. She dropped to his side. "How are you feeling?"

His gaze slid to her. "Bessie?"

Lillian slipped her hand in her pocket and fingered the ribbon. "Is Bessie your wife?"

He swallowed. "Water…"

She fetched him a cup and helped him drink. "Who is Bessie?"

He took a long gulp and laid back on his bedroll. "My girl."

My girl? Was he referring to a wife or daughter? She pulled the ribbon from her pocket and held it up so he could get a look at it. "It this hers?"

His eyes widened. "Bessie, you here?"

"No, she's not. I'm Lillian Gardner—Doctor Gardner. Who is Bessie?" She hoped not a child. "Do you recall what happened when you were dragging the log?"

He shook his head. "Where's my Bessie?" He closed his eyes.

"She's not here. Who am I looking for? A girl or a woman?"

He lay still.

"Mister," Lillian said. "Is she here with you?" She gently shook his shoulder. He opened his eyes, glanced around, and closed them. Where could she be? She went to the accident site and hollered, "Bessie!" Walking around, she tried to find any sign of another person and found none. There was only the ribbon.

Lillian assumed Bessie was a woman back home waiting for him. All she had to do was figure out where home was. And to do that, she needed to get him to the village.

After finding the sugar sack, Lillian went back to Shorty. She tossed the sack against his hide until he stood quietly with it slapping him. Then led him to a pole. She found a stick on the ground and rubbed his body with it before lifting one side of the pole in the air. He flinched but remained in place. "That's a good boy." She massaged his neck and back, examining more wounds. Since they looked fine, she continued with the poles. She tried to reach his back to hook him to the travois, but he was too tall. She led Shorty to one of the logs and stepped up, dragged the sledge behind him, and hooked the travois to leather straps.

When she was satisfied the man's mobile stick bed was secure, she hopped off the log and led the horse forward. Shorty spooked and ran sideways. One of the poles snapped, causing the big gelding to drag the fractured travois behind him. Lillian released the rope, not wanting more burns. She picked up a pinecone and flung it at the horse's behind, shouting, "You wretched beast! Come back here!"

She plopped down on the log she used as a step-stool and hid her face in her hands. "What do you want me to do, Lord?" She didn't want to stay there. Alone. With him. She needed the healer's wisdom.

When calm, she pushed herself from the log and fetched Shorty. "You have to work with me, boy." He rubbed his massive head on her shoulder and she side-stepped. She laughed and rubbed his nose before unhooking the mangled mess of poles and led him to the creek for a drink. When he was more than waist-deep, she crawled on his back, spread her water-logged skirt over his back, and rubbed him all over.

He took a few steps, looked back at her, and meandered downstream, veering toward the bank. She let him go where he pleased, talking to him in a comforting voice. As Lillian hummed, she realized she was acting like both her mother and Hannah. "I must be more like them than I realize," she told Shorty, feeling heavy just thinking about them. The wedding, Hannah's snide remarks, Delbert chasing after her. She shook her head and reined the brown giant back to the campsite.

Moans pulsed from the lean-to. Lillian slid off Shorty and rushed into the shelter. The heat stifled her breathing. Beads of sweat covered his forehead. "I should have paid more attention to you..." She rummaged through his belongings and pulled a couple of shirts from a tattered trunk, trudged to the river, her heavy skirt slowing her down, and dunked the shirts into the water. Back at camp, she laid one shirt over his chest, patted his head and neck with the second shirt, and then laid it over the crown of his head.

The doctor's satchel and her buckskin pouch perched on the ground. She fetched them both and gave him a dose of morphine for pain and willow bark for fever. Lillian realized she needed to study the medicines at greater length. She examined his leg, noting the splint was in place, and dragged him and his bedroll out of the lean-to and into the shade of pine trees.

Her tummy groaned, so she found hardtack and dried meat of some type and devoured it, washing it all down with a swig of water. She dug around and found coffee beans and a grinder and made herself a cup of coffee as the heat and exertion were making her tired. She needed the energy as she feared she would need to transport the man back to Fort Colville and Doctor Harris.

Perhaps Yellow Owl would come with her.

Once Lillian had a couple of cups of coffee in her, she repaired the travois, attached the long poles to Shorty's harness, and got him walking without spooking. In a way, she now understood her sister's love of horses. After working with Shorty and getting him settled into the harness and travois, she felt a connection with the gentle giant.

A crunch and snap sounded in the distance. A flock of shivers raced across Lillian's back and she stood, her eyes narrow.

Yellow Owl appeared on a spotted horse from the shadows of trees and buckbrush. Lillian sighed, her shoulders sagging. "Hello, friend. I'm happy you have come."

Lillian tipped her head. "My, how your flawless English has suddenly appeared."

Yellow Owl blushed. "It is our way to trust you before we let you into our inner circle. You have proved yourself."

"Inner circle?" Lillian wanted to be agitated, but there was no time.

Yellow Owl motioned to the draft horse. "Beaver Head's annoyance made me think you needed help."

"He seems to think I can do this by myself."

"You are correct, and I too am sure you can. But still, I would like to help. Four hands are better than two." Yellow Owl slid off her horse. "What do you want me to do?"

"I don't know much about the fellow, but he's in a bad way." Lillian told her friend what she knew and her wish to get him back to Fort Colville. "If there is a way, can you come with me?"

Yellow Owl shook her head. "The mountain pass you crossed to get here is still on fire. The trails are blocked until it snows." She held up a hand. "Have you not noticed the ash and haze in the sky?"

"Of course I have." Lillian sighed. "There has to be another way." In the distance, plumes of smoke filled the northern horizon.

"There is one, but it will take many sunrises. Too many."

"But he needs a surgeon." Lillian pointed to him. "Look at him, he needs medical attention."

"You are a doctor. You fix him."

191

Tears stung her eyes. She dabbed at them. "I have only studied for a short time under Doctor Maddox. I don't know enough to help him."

"I will help you get him to our village. That is all."

Lillian nodded. "Let's get him loaded." The girls secured the man in the travois, rounded up their horses, and headed north.

CHAPTER 30

Lillian found a quiet spot near her campsite and opened her journal. She took a sip of water, soothing her scratchy throat.

Beaver Head was wrong. I cannot do this by myself. Yellow Owl had to help me. I know in my heart he recognized that I am somewhat of a swindler and that is the actual reason he walked away from us. I feel I can no longer refer to myself as a doctor. I have lied to myself and those in my path.

My training is limited. I understand little with what slight time I have had with Mali. Mama's methods are most familiar to me. I am more comfortable with the Indian medicines than Doctor Maddox's remedies. She had proper training under her husband. Today proved I must stop acting like a healer. I am far from qualified.

I must learn of a path home and leave as soon as I can. Beaver Head can tend to the man. I can only pray he heals and finds his Bessie.

I will have to find another way to leave a legacy of hope. Perhaps in my continued methods of healing with plants. There is much to learn. Mama was right, we all have a place in this world, but we sometimes have to dig in the soil to discover it.

Lillian Gardner, a natural healer, might suit me better. I can harvest local plants and roots and take them around to homesteads and make sure everyone has plenty of medicines. I can at least soothe their souls.

She went back to her tent, found her stethoscope, and turned it over in her hands. She rummaged through all of Mali's medicines and found a couple of medical books. Cracking the texts open, she scoured through their pages. Some of the remedies seemed so simple. Yet much of it overwhelmed her. She set the books on her bed and picked up her journal. The pages opened to: *We must leave a legacy of hope.* She clung to the reminder as she ran a finger over the words. Could she do it? Become a woman doctor like Mali? Combine both forms of medicines?

Lillian clutched Mali's scarf to her chest and penned:

Someday I will find one of these schools for medicine and enroll. I will find a way for them to accept me. She would do it in honor of her deceased companion.

CHAPTER 31

Five days later, Lillian said her goodbyes to the River Paddlers, rolled the hide map Chief Victor had drawn for her and Mali, and hugged Yellow Owl.

"I will miss you," Lillian said. "You are a faithful friend."

Yellow Owl handed her a parfleche. "This will get you home. If you ride fast, you will be home soon."

Lillian untied the stiff bag and peeked inside to find camas cakes, dried fish and small game, various roots and dried berries, and bannock. She embraced Yellow Owl for a long moment. "Thank you, my friend." She tied the bag to Chwim's saddle and untied her bag of herbs.

Yellow Owl came beside her and pressed a hand on Lillian's, shaking her head. "You have already given us much. No more."

Lillian inhaled a warm breath and nodded. She tied the pouch back on Asa's saddle. "I hope to see you again someday."

"I would like that."

Lillian mounted Asa, Chwim in tow. "Thank you for agreeing to help Bessie when she arrives." She was thankful the man, Frank Goodman, was talking and gaining strength. To find out Bessie was his bride-to-be and where she lived was a relief. The greatest reprieve was knowing she didn't need to haul Mr. Goodman over the mountain on a travois.

"It will be good for them to reunite." Yellow Owl waved. "Safe travels."

As Lillian rode along the Pend Oreille River, she imagined her reunion with her folks. Hugs, a hearty meal, stories of her experiences. She shoved thoughts of fear, guilt, and doubt from her mind, wanting to concentrate on a joyous reunion. She craved to know if they'd received word on how Hannah and Leslie were settling in. She even desired to go to the Sinyekst village to see Spupaleena and talk with the healer, Simillkameen, while the old woman's mind and eyes were still sharp. Hopefully, the woman would agree to teach Lillian alongside her mother.

Even though she was thrilled to be going home, her chest felt heavy. Lillian knew she'd have to explain herself. She sighed. The right words would come in time. She was thankful there were plenty of miles between them to decide what to say.

Heat enveloped her and the valley as the sun rested on the eastern mountains, making its usual morning climb. The reflections on the water were as hazy as the sky overhead. She hoped the trail to what the River Paddlers referred to as S che wee leh, or water snake, would be without trials.

It was late afternoon when Lillian stopped for a break before starting over the pass leading to the S che wee leh settlement. The hide map on her lap, she was trying to figure out where to camp for the night when a man approached. Her belly rolled at the sight of the dark, beady-eyed fella and his bushy appearance. He must have been in his late thirties, she guessed, and seemed familiar.

"Permission to approach your camp." He tipped his black cowboy hat on the back of his head, untied his neckerchief, and mopped his brow, giving her a toothless grin.

Then it hit her. This was the fella who was staring at her at Fort Colville. Shudders scampered down her spine. Her pistol. Darn, it was in her saddlebag. But her knife was in her boot. She forced herself to remain calm, fighting the panic beckoning her.

No one was around to help her. She should have insisted on having an escort. Lillian wanted to turn down his request, yet she feared if she did, harm—even death—would come to her, so she nodded, her body trembling.

"I'm obliged, ma'am."

His genteel manners conflicted with his outlaw presence. She sat up, trying to appear confident, her breaths increasing. Was he a hardworking man in need of rest and nourishment or a desperado tending to do who knows what to her?

"What's a young filly like you doing out here alone?" He dismounted and stood over her as though intending to frighten her.

Lillian swallowed a lump clogging her throat. What on earth would he want with her? "I—huh..." Two six-guns hugged his scrawny hips. A rifle hung from under the right fender of his worn saddle. She wondered if his fit gray horse was stolen. How could a man looking so shabby have such a well-groomed mount? Blinking several times, she said, "I've come from the village upriver."

He studied her, the two geldings, and her packs. "Why you got two horses?"

"My companion, Doctor Maddox passed away." She wrung her hands, her belly feeling queasy.

"You some kinda healer, girly?"

"In a way."

"What were you and the old lady doing outside Fort Colville?"

"I—um—I was studying medicine with the doctor."

"Whatcha doing over here?"

"We came to help…" Any more questions and she figured she'd retch. *Why won't he leave me alone?*

"Figured so when I seen you ladies at the fort. You can imagine my surprise seeing you sittin' here." He rolled up his sleeve and exposed a rather long gash on his arm. "I need you to stitch this up." He leaned to the side to spit a stream of brown juice from his mouth.

Had he been following them? The thought made her dizzy. Lillian slowly nodded, willing her body to move. Perhaps if she did what he asked, he'd be on his way. She rolled up her map and secured it in her pouch. She reached for the medical satchel. Her pistol was on one side of the horse, and her medical bag was on the other. How could she distract him and get to it?

"What's takin' you so long?"

"I need my herbs. They're in the saddlebag on the other side of my horse."

"You don't need no herbs to stitch my arm." He waved a six-shooter in the air and took a few steps toward her. "Get over here, now!" He pointed the gun at her chest.

Her hands shaking, she untied the medical bag and brought it over to where she had been sitting. A needle poked her finger when she rummaged around the bag. She bit her bottom lip, not about to show him any sign of weakness.

198

"Hurry up!"

She fished through the bag, searching for thread. When she didn't find any, she moved to the pack tied to Asa's saddle horn.

"Whatcha doin' over there?" He put a hand on one of his guns.

"Trying to find thread."

"Don't you go tryin' anything, now, girly."

"Doctor Gardner, if you please."

He laughed. "Doctor, huh? I thought you said you were kind of a healer. Are ya a doctor or not?"

Lillian caught his gaze. "Yes, mister, I am." She found a spool, threaded the needle, and turned to him. "This won't take long."

He pulled back his arm. "Ain't ya gonna clean my cut first?"

She took in a deep breath through her nose, feeling her nostrils flare. "Suppose I should."

"Seems to me you need more schoolin'."

"Like I said, my companion died." Behind him, something caught her attention. She tried to watch the trees without making a fuss.

"You sure you can fix me up?"

Lillian smiled. "Mama taught me to quilt. Not much difference poking a needle through fabric or flesh." She dug a scrap of flannel and antiseptic solution from the satchel, wiped blood from his arm, and stuck the needle in deep.

"Ow!" He flinched. "Watch it, missy."

A small smile on her face, Lillian stitched his gash, not taking her time to be gentle, hoping it stung the ruthless man. She sewed the inside layers first, working her way to the skin while keeping an eye on him. Each stitch was tight and small. *Mama would be proud.*

From where she'd seen the earlier movement, a boy about Lillian's age brandished his face from behind a tree. She shook her head without causing the outlaw to notice. Who was he? Thankfully, the ruffian's eyes were averted and he was babbling on about her fixing him up so he could be on his way. But would he let her go?

Brush moved and a younger girl's face popped up, her eyes round. Lillian felt herself stiffen. Who were they? Surely the pair was not with the menace she was working on. Were there more of them? Why were they there? Where were they from? The boy motioned for the girl to take cover. He put a finger to his lips and disappeared behind the tree. Lillian took in a deep breath to steady her fingers. Where were their folks? Did they need help?

As she sewed his arm, she hoped he'd leave so she'd be done with him. *Those two had better stay put.* So far, so good. There was no sign of the two hiding in the trees. Were they lost? She shook her head and began to softly hum to steady her nerves. Prayed God would protect her from any mischievous intentions running through his mind. She tied a couple of knots and cut the thread. "That'll do." She wiped the needle with antiseptic solution and a clean piece of flannel and put away her medical supplies. "Suppose you'll be moving on."

He grabbed her shoulders and tried to kiss her. She turned her head, pulled away, and slapped his face. "Get away from me!"

He lunged at her.

"Leave her alone!" the young man said as he pulled him off Lillian.

The outlaw spun around, slamming his forearm into the boy's face, sending him backward. Lillian slipped her knife from her boot and held it out. "Don't touch him!"

"Well, lookie here." The outlaw smiled, showing brown-stained teeth. "What have we got? Two more little ones! They belong to you, girly?"

"Yep, that makes three to one," the girl said as she leveled a rifle at his face.

The young man strode to Lillian. "You all right?"

Lillian nodded. "He was just leavin'." She narrowed her eyes.

The outlaw spat on the ground, scowled at Lillian, mounted, and sped away.

The girl, tall and thin, wearing a cowboy hat with a string tied under her chin, rushed to Lillian's side, rifle in hand. "You sure you're all right?"

Lillian nodded. "Glad you two showed up when you did. I had a bad feeling about that man. Seems like an outlaw to me."

"Who is he?" The young man's gaze followed the ruffian.

"Not sure. I first saw him back at Fort Colville then he came out of nowhere when I was studying a map. I stitched his gash. Guess I should have paid more attention." Lillian shook her head. "I'm Lillian Gardner."

"I'm Olive Watts and this here's my brother, Simon." Simon tipped his hat at Lillian. "You some kinda doctor?"

"Kinda young, ain't ya?" Simon studied Lillian, making her feel uncomfortable.

Lillian figured Simon was around her age, and Olive a year or two younger. "More of a healer," she said, noticing how reedy the pair looked. "I was studying with a Welsh doctor until she recently passed away. I'm headed home. You two hungry?" She motioned to the packs. "I have some rations."

The siblings looked at each other, and Olive nodded. "Sure are."

Lillian grabbed a parfleche of food and a couple of canteens and spread a quilt over a patch of sunburned grass. She motioned for them to join her on the coverlet. "Where you from?"

"What is this?" Olive picked up a camas cake.

"The River Paddler's gave it to me."

"The who?" Simon's brows furrowed.

"They're a village of Indians a few miles north of here." Lillian took a swig from the canteen and passed it to Olive. "Where you headed?"

Olive shrugged. "We're…" She glanced at her brother.

"From Kansas," Simon said. "We're still decidin' where to settle."

Lillian nodded. "Beautiful country in these parts. Where're your folks?"

Olive's gaze shot to her brother and she shook her head. Simon studied his sister for a brief moment. "I think we can trust her," he said and turned to Lillian. "They died a few days ago. We found the perfect spot to homestead with plenty of fish and game. A creek ran past the cabin Pa and I were buildin'. This land is rich for farming. They were so excited…"

Olive sniffed and wiped her eyes, doing her best to appear strong.

"Oh, goodness." Lillian pressed a hand to her throat. "Sorry for your loss. How'd they pass?"

"They, uh…" Simon's voice hitched. "Pa was fixing a leak in the roof. Mama had gone up to give him more nails and slipped. Pa tried to catch her arm, but…" He wiped his eyes. "They both rolled off. Pa hit his head and, well, Mama looks like she might have broken her neck."

"Mama had no business being on the roof." Olive glared at her brother.

His cheeks pinked. "Pa sent me to hunt that morning. We were almost out of food. Had a few potatoes, beans, coffee…"

Lillian motioned to the rations. "Help yourself. There's plenty."

Simon picked up a hunk of dried meat and tore off a piece with his teeth.

"I'm headed to S che wee leh just over this pass. You're welcome to come along." Lillian crossed her ankles.

Olive nodded at Simon. "It's settled then," Lillian said. "I'm grateful for the company."

After the Wattses filled their bellies, Lillian packed their supplies and rearranged bags. Lillian mounted Asa, and the siblings rode Chwim. They trekked for several miles up the mountain and stopped for the night.

Simon watered the horses while the girls made camp. When satisfied, Lillian found her journal and opened it.

CHAPTER 32

August 23

Thank the good Lord the Wattses rescued me from the outlaw drifter! I do not know what I would have done had they not come. Mercy. I pray he either turns from his wild ways or gets put under. Forgive me, Lord, for my ill thoughts toward him. Thank you for sending Olive and Simon to intervene. My heart hurts for them, losing their folks so young.

Then again, thank you for sending them to me so I do not have to travel alone. Forgive my selfishness. Truth be told, it was frightening to think I would have to cross the pass by myself. Even if the Indian trails are well suited, men like that drifter I stitched today prey on young ladies like me. I pray we are rid of him and any other ruffians on the journey.

I cannot wait to get home and see my family. Feel safe on our homestead.

I miss Yellow Owl. She was becoming like a sister to me. The kind of sister I hoped to have someday. She and I had so much more in common than Hannah and I do. I love my sister, but it is hard to talk with her about the things I dream about and hope for.

I pray Frank heals and he and Bessie reunite soon. Yellow Owl will be a fine friend to her. I hope Bessie will be hardy enough to live in this harsh country.

It is said when we crown the mountain, we will be able to see for miles. I hope so. The rivers, lakes, and valleys are truly created from the hand of God. What a spectacular mystery it all is.

I shall get rest as it will be a long day of travel off the mountain tomorrow. If we make it that far. I can only hope that evil man is far from us.

Lillian squinted against the darkness, shadows hindering her view. She put the journal away and settled in for the night. As her eyelids grew heavy, she felt the urge to be on guard.

CHAPTER 33

A snap, like footsteps on twigs, made Lillian shoot upright. Whose feet made the noise, she was unsure. She blinked her heavy eyelids open. A black form and the outline of a six-shooter hovered over her. She gasped as a calloused hand covered her mouth, pushing her back down.

"You got some medicine I need," the man whispered.

Lillian recognized the outlaw's voice, his pungent breath on the side of her face. She thrashed and screamed, his hand muffling the noise.

He grabbed her by the hair and pulled her to her feet. "Shut up!" he said. "Or I'll kill your friends."

Lillian kicked a pinecone toward Olive, hitting her in the foot. "Mmm…" The girl shifted. Lillian kicked another cone at her and missed.

"What're you doin'?" The outlaw shook her.

Lillian lost her balance, slammed into him, and fell. She grabbed hold of Simon's legs. He woke with a start and kicked her in the face. She screamed. "He's back!"

Simon sprang to his feet and tackled the man. While they wrestled on the ground, Lillian woke up Olive and tugged her upright. A shot split the air, a man groaned, and a thud hit the ground.

"Simon!" Olive hollered as she scrambled to her feet. But Lillian got to her before the girl had a chance to get to him and pulled her back down.

"Be quiet or he'll come after us," she whispered to the scared girl. Lillian felt Olive tremble as she held onto her arm. "Sshhh. Don't worry, we'll get out of this." She prayed they would.

The outlaw rolled Simon off him, stood, and pointed the pistol at the girls. "Show me your satchel," he said to Lillian.

Lillian cocked her head. "Which one?"

"Don't sass me, girly." He again dragged her to her feet by her hair and flung her around, thrusting her toward the saddles.

"Leave her alone!" Olive stood, her eyes wide.

He pointed the gun at Olive. "Don't try anything or you'll end up like him." He jerked his head toward Simon's body.

"Why did you have to kill my brother? We've done nothing to you!"

"Shut up!" The outlaw took a step toward Olive, and she simmered. "You wait there while we get the doctor's bag."

Lillian took a shaky step toward the saddles and retrieved the satchel. He grabbed it out of her hand and opened it. "Now saddle your horses." He waved his gun at the girls.

"I can't leave without burying my brother." Olive wiped her eyes with the back of her hand.

Olive's sobs ripped through Lillian. The poor girl, first her parents and now her brother. It appeared they had no other family. If they did, they must not reside close, or they'd be there and not in the mountains with her and the grizzled outlaw. Simon would be alive.

Lillian swallowed the bile rising in her throat. She needed to keep them both safe. Olive deserved a future. Her ma would surely take in the girl, welcome her like another daughter.

"We ain't got time for that."

Lillian signaled for Olive to get the rifle. The girl gave a small nod.

"What do you want out of the satchel?" Lillian said to distract the outlaw. "Maybe I can help you find it."

Olive went for the gun. The man dropped the satchel and six-shooter, snagged the rifle out of Olive's hands, and clobbered her over the head with the butt of his weapon. She dropped to the ground and groaned, holding her head. Lillian ran to Olive's side, the outlaw leveling the rifle at her head.

"What're you thinkin'?" The man picked up his pistol and holstered it, made sure the rifle was loaded. "You girlies better watch yourselves, now. Might get hurt." He spat a long stream of brown juice from his mouth, studied Lillian. "You ain't no healer, are ya? Why, I bet you killed the doctor who owned that there horse and stole her belongings. Looks like I'll have to drag you both to the first sheriff we come across." He gave Lillian a lopsided grin. "Maybe I should save myself some time and hang you myself for stealin' horses and impersonatin' a doctor."

Lillian swallowed hard. She bet he was the one who was wanted by the law and felt he was bluffing. "You know I didn't kill nobody, and I didn't steal Chw—those horses." She pursed her lips.

"Now, little lady. I don't think lyin's a hanging offense, but…" He cackled. "There are other ways we can rectify this here situation." He ran a slimy finger down her jawline.

Lillian kicked him as hard as she could. He buckled over and dropped the rifle, his face as red as an apple. Lillian scrambled to recover it and stood tall, pointing the gun at his head. "I think there's a law to hang swindlers like you." She motioned to a thick fir with the rifle, then swung the weapon toward his belt. "Drop that other pistol on the ground, kick it over here, and go on over there." She motioned to a sturdy Ponderosa Pine. "Olive, get the rope out of the saddlebag Chwim packed."

The man slid the gun out of its holster and tossed it on the ground.

"Who?"

"The horse you rode." Lillian picked up the six-shooter.

"Oh…" Olive found a hemp rope and brought it to Lillian.

"Get against the tree." Lillian blinked sweat out of her eyes. When the ruffian was on his rear, his back to the trunk, she told Olive, "Go ahead and tie him up."

Olive wound the rope three times around the tree. "I can't get it tight enough."

Lillian gave her the rifle. "Don't take it off him." Olive nodded while Lillian tightened and knotted the rope.

The man laughed and said, "Don't fall asleep, girlies. I'll get outta this and come after you. You'll be dead before dawn."

Lillian's gut twisted as she pointed the rifle at the outlaw. "Try anything and you'll drop before I can blink." She gave one six-shooter to Olive. "Keep this in case you need it." She sat against a tamarack and laid the rifle across her lap. "Go on back to bed, Olive. I'll take first watch." She made sure the pistol was loaded. It was one bullet short.

"Wake up."

Lillian's eyes sprang open. Olive's face was in hers. She pushed the girl back. "What is it?" She clutched the cold metal and wood of the rifle.

"He's gone!" Olive pulled Lillian to her feet. "Looks like he cut the rope and fled with the satchel."

Lillian shook her head, turning in a circle. "I think we need to pack our belongings and head farther up the mountain. We can't stay here."

"Either way he'll find us," Olive said. "I know how to make small game traps. I could set a large snare or two."

"That's a good idea, but we don't know if he's hiding in the trees, watching us, or if he's gone. Besides, I don't think we have enough rope."

Olive slouched.

"Don't worry. We'll get him first. Let's pack up and hit the trail."

The girls saddled their horses and headed west. When near the top of the pass and sure the outlaw was not following them, they stopped to rest. While Olive untied the bedrolls, Lillian rode a small perimeter, searching for any sign of the outlaw. Even at high elevations, the heat made them sweat. Lillian unhooked her canteen. She groaned.

"What's wrong?" Olive resembled a wilted wildflower.

"I forgot to fill up the canteens. There's only a bit of water in mine. You got any?"

Olive shook her canteen. "Don't think so."

"Here, you drink this."

Olive took a swig. "We can share. You need some too."

Lillian took a small drink and capped the canteen. "We need to rest awhile." She studied the girl. "You've been through enough. I'll keep watch. He's probably gone by now. He has what he wanted."

"What do you think he'll do with the medication?"

"Who knows? Sell it. Use it. There's a lot of crooked people in the world."

"Do you think someone he knows needs help?"

Lillian shrugged. "Maybe. I doubt it though. Renegades like him don't care about others." She motioned to a patch of grass. "Go get some rest. I'll wake you after a spell." Olive settled with her back to Lillian. Soft sobs came from the girl, her shoulders shaking.

CHAPTER 34

August 25

Lillian settled in the shade with her journal. Tears blurred her vision as she thought about Simon's death and Olive's future. She sketched them, the village, both mountain passes, the fire, Owen, and the outlaw, wondering if they'd make it out alive.

Dear Heavenly Father, I pray you keep that wretched man away from us. Give us safe passage off this mountain. What more could he want? He's got the satchel.

The answer made her belly flip. She closed her eyes for a moment before taking a shaky hand to paper.

I had looked forward to traveling with the Wattses. Simon and his way of making us feel protected. Olive and her jovial nature. Their fun sibling banter. I could tell they were close. Had to depend on one another after their folks' death. They remind me of Delbert and Hannah. Unfortunately, this leg of the journey has been a nightmare. What do we do now? I wish Pa was here to protect us. I've never been so frightened in my life.

Lillian choked back a sob.

I intend to ask Mama if Olive can be part of our family. I am certain she will agree. She is a wonderful soul—

Lillian's pen hovered over the page, her ear cocked. The sound of leaves crunching underfoot made her gasp.

CHAPTER 35

"I've come back for ya, girly!" The outlaw showed his face, his eyes bloodshot. He looked like he hadn't slept in days. Lillian was sure he'd ingested some medications from the satchel, but why? Which ones?

Lillian sprang to her feet, dropping the journal and pen, and went for her gun. She pulled the trigger and all it did was click. She tried again. Nothing. She stuck it into the pocket of her skirt and froze.

"Get up." He motioned to Olive. "And wake her up. Time to come with me." He waved a pistol at her.

The gun was new. Lillian wondered who he'd stolen it from. She swallowed the rock in her throat, knowing he'd probably killed some poor soul for it. She went to Olive and shook the girl's shoulder. "Get up." She leaned close. "He's back. Get up and don't say a thing. Stick close to me."

Olive nodded.

"I need the rifle off Asa. Try to distract him and I'll get it."

Olive again nodded and eased to her feet.

Lillian faced him. "Now what?"

"Me, you," he said, "and a couple of my friends are gonna have us a little party."

Lillian wanted to slap the smirk off his face. "I don't see anyone else."

"They ain't far from here."

"How'd you get here?" Olive said. "I don't see no horse."

"Got him tied up over yonder."

"Where's your friends?" Olive glanced over his shoulder, trying to stay upright on wobbly legs. "What kind of party you have in mind?" She tried to keep her voice soft and pleasing.

He gave her a greasy smile.

Olive frowned. "I don't have nothing to bake a cake with." Her gaze dropped to the ground, her bottom lip protruding. She crossed her arms over her chest and rocked side to side.

Lillian smiled, snuck over to Asa, and retrieved the six-shooter. *If Olive keeps up this act, we may have a chance.*

"I like cake." He strode to Olive and took her by the arm. "Maybe if I find you the fixin's for one you can bake it." He scoffed. "Hey, boys, this one's gonna bake us a cake!"

What a fool! Lillian knew he was alone, him being an awful actor and all. She crept closer and leveled the gun at him. "Not sure she'll be baking anything for you anytime soon."

He whirled around, his gun pointed at Lillian. Then grabbed Olive and pressed the barrel to her head. "You don't want me to kill her, now, do ya, girly?"

"You shoot her, I'll drop you, mister." Lillian took a few steps closer. "You got your remedies, what more do you want?"

"That's no way to talk to a gentleman—"

216

"Gentleman! Don't see one of them," Lillian said. "I do see a no-account polecat though. Right before my eyes." She waved the gun at him. "Let her go."

With Olive in tow, he went around Lillian and the horses. "You should have listened to me. Now I'm gonna have to kill this one."

"Lillian!" Olive struggled against his hold.

"Do what he says, Olive," Lillian said. "I won't let him hurt you." She kept her six-shooter pinned between his eyes.

The outlaw rushed off, dragging Olive with him. Lillian reloaded both six-shooters and checked the rifle, untied Chwim, and jumped on Asa. She tore out after them, knowing she had to stop him from reaching any other men and their horses, believing he may not have been bluffing. Otherwise Olive would surely die.

But she didn't find them. They had a short head start on her. *Where could they have gone?* She searched for caves, hollowed tree trunks, anywhere they might be hiding.

After a while, she rode back to where they stopped to rest and followed their tracks. She came to where their footprints connected with hoof prints. She circled the sets of prints and slid off her horse. There was only one set of horse prints. She chortled. "I should have trusted my gut."

Lillian followed the prints on foot, finding they circled back toward the village. She mounted Asa and started down the mountain, headed for the Pend Oreille.

Dusk clouded Lillian's vision. "I have to keep going!" She reined Asa to a stop and dropped the reins. The horses would need water soon. They dropped their heads and grazed. She studied the grounds, looking for any sign she could find.

Several feet from her was a pile of horse dung. She toed it with the tip of her boot. "Somewhat fresh." She chewed on her bottom lip. "Gotta find her soon," she whispered.

Lillian lifted the canteen from the saddle horn and swirled it around, wetting her aching lips. Olive would need the rest. After looping the canteen back over the horn, she went in search of dried berries. Locating some, she plopped a handful in her mouth. They would have to do for now. Her body cried for food and rest, but she couldn't take the time. Not until Olive was safe.

An owl hooted overhead. According to Sinyekst lore, the bird meant death was looming. She shivered. No way was it going to be the girl. An image of the oily bandit slid across Lillian's mind. She fetched a hunk of dried salmon from one of her packs and tore off a piece with her teeth. She stroked Asa's neck. "We have to find her." He rubbed her shoulder with the side of his face.

She took hold of the horses' ropes. "Come on, boys. Let's go get her." She mounted Asa and tugged on Chwim's lead rope. With each snap of a twig or crunch of dried leaves, Lillian cringed. She'd have to wait until they were asleep to go in and retrieve her.

The moon glimmered through the trees that night, casting haunting shadows over his camp. Smoke wafted through the trees. Was he that big of an idiot to light a fire? Or was it a trap?

Lillian waited. She'd found his camp and tied the horses several yards away so they couldn't be detected. Faint flames glowed near a dark form the size of a man. Where was Olive?

She took a few steps closer, her fingers wrapped around the cool metal of the six-shooters, remembering the owl's hoot.

A pinecone rolled under her foot, and she stepped off balance. Leaves crunched as she regained her footing. Her steps too loud, she eased to the ground and slipped off her boots, tied them together, and hung them over a low branch. She crept forward. A lengthy form shifted. It was too long to be either of them.

Lillian felt a hard object jab her back.

"Told ya we're gonna have us a party, girly," he whispered.

His warm breath made her recoil. She spun around and kicked him in the gut. He groaned and dropped.

"Watch out!" Olive shouted.

Lillian sank to the ground, trying to find the girl. The crack of a rifle rang through the air, and a bullet whizzed past her head. She closed her eyes, stiffened. To her left, footsteps scampered and stopped. To her right, a man on the ground groaned and rolled to his feet, a pistol out and ready to shoot.

She lay prone, keeping her breaths soft and shallow. She pointed one gun at the greenhorn on her left and one on the staggering outlaw on the right. *Where's Olive?*

"Do ya see 'er?" the man on the left said.

"Shut up!" The outlaw waved his sidearm around.

Lillian squinted at the man on the left. She'd have to get the outlaw first. He was closer. The other one seemed dumber, but she could deal with him later. She needed to know if there were more of them out there.

The outlaw took a step toward her. She recalled how her father had taught her to aim and hold the weapon so it wouldn't jerk to the side. She sucked in a breath, held it, and pulled the trigger. The shot rang in her ears, and he toppled to the ground. The man on the left hollered, racing toward her. She leveled the gun at him and squeezed the trigger.

"Owww!" He tripped and fell a few feet from Lillian. "She got me!"

He was at an odd angle, and Lillian couldn't get a good shot at him. The kill shot she knew she needed for survival.

"Seth, you see 'er?"

Seth? Lillian was glad to know the name of the man she'd just saved women from. She scooted to the side.

"I'll get ya!" The man pushed to his feet and took a wobbly step, his gun waving at her.

Lillian closed an eye, aimed, and squeezed the trigger. The recoil startled her. The man dropped. She scrambled to her feet. "Olive, where are you? Are there any more of them?"

"No more. I'm over here." Her voice meandered through the trees.

Lillian tipped her head. "Sing or something so I can find you."

"I'm scared."

"Just do it!"

"She came and rescued me," Olive sang in a low tone, her voice wavering. "Like she said she would. And now the two swindlers are dead. She shot them down…"

Lillian followed the voice and found Olive tied to a tree. She dropped to her knees and hugged the girl. "You're safe now," she said. Lillian untied her.

Olive rubbed her wrists, sniffing.

"Did they hurt you?"

Olive shook her head.

"You sure there are no more?"

"I only saw two of them. Seth called the other one 'Dodger.' "

"Okay, let's get their horses and supplies and get out of here."

The girls packed bedrolls and other food and supplies and the medical satchel and tied them to the two horses they found nearby. The medicines and stethoscope seemed okay, which made her think he intended to sell them, but she would have to examine the contents in the light of day.

"You ever lead a horse from the saddle before?" Lillian said.

"Yeah, plenty of times." Olive took one of the horses from Lillian.

"Good, let's get up the mountain and make camp."

"I just as soon keep going. I'm not tired."

"Good. Me either."

The girls rode most of the night, letting the horses pick their way through trees and down a rugged trail. Near the bottom, Olive slid to the side and caught the saddle horn. "Maybe we should stop for a spell." The sun would be up soon.

"Okay." Lillian rubbed her eyes. They untied bedrolls, secured horses, and bedded down for a few hours of shut-eye.

CHAPTER 36

August 26

Lillian could not get the scene out of her head. She yawned and rubbed her eyes, afraid to sleep. Her mouth was as dry as a waterless creek. She blinked a few times and touched her fountain pen to paper. Olive was curled up in her bedroll, her body touching Lillian's. Lillian figured the girl's thoughts were as jumbled as hers.

God, I hope you can forgive me for killing those men.

Her hands shook as she tried to write.

I figured it was either us or them. It was a miracle the bullets made their mark and dropped the outlaws. I'm still shaking.

She wiped her eyes, reminding herself to breathe.

It had to be you protecting us. There is no other explanation. I figure I owe you my life. Olive's too. I wish you would have spared Simon. But I suppose you have your reasons for taking him.

I'm not sure this medical journey is worth it. Perhaps this is my punishment for leaving like I did. I hope you can forgive me for all my awful deeds. Hope Mama and Pa can forgive me too. I am so sorry for what I've done. So very sorry.

Please let us make it home. I miss my family so much my heart feels like it is being ripped straight out of my chest.

Lillian wiped her eyes with the sleeve of her shirtwaist.

In the next few hours we should be to S che wee leh. I'm so thirsty. My head aches, and my vision is blurred. But I will hide these symptoms from Olive as I am certain it is from fatigue and dehydration. I do not wish to scare her any more than she already is.

During the night, Olive screamed in her sleep. I fear she is reliving her brother's death and her kidnapping in her dreams. If only we could have had time and tools to bury Simon. I pray the outlaws did not harm her in any way. If so, I fear she may never recover with the loss of her family. Oh Lord, ease her mind. Let her know she is safe. The poor girl. Her life will never be the same. Tell me what to say. How to comfort her. Give her a peace that surpasses all understanding. Give her the strength to carry on.

Olive lay in a bedroll, her breaths shallow. She looked peaceful. Lillian wiped her face with her neckerchief. They had to make it back to her folks.

I plan to head straight home to Pa and Mama and Delbert. There is nothing more I want to see or do. I have helped all I can for now. I fear I won't sleep tonight. I am terrified to close my eyes.

I need to get Olive water and a meal that will stick to her ribs. She is a fighter, and I admire her will to live.

We will have one mountain to climb before reaching the Columbia. Hopefully, God will lead me to someone who can draw me another map.

Lillian sketched the map Chief Victor had given her in her journal before losing light. She sketched the wildflowers they'd come across over the mountains. Anything to keep her mind busy and give her a smidgen of hope.

This journey was not what I expected and one I pray I never take again. The only good that has come from it are the friends I have made along the way. Especially with Doctor Maddox, God rest her soul, and Yellow Owl. For them, I am humbled and thankful as they have blessed and enriched my life.

Now, to find folks who will help us.

Chapter 37

A two-story house with a peaked roof emerged in the distance. Coral honeysuckle vines climbed a side of the house. The open porch welcomed Lillian. A handful of young'uns romped inside a picket fence. "Let's stop here."

Olive nodded as she watched the children play. A well-groomed woman came from inside the house. "Welcome!" She wiped her hands on her apron.

Lillian dismounted. "Good day, ma'am. We're looking for a place to rest."

"Oh, my," the woman said, "you both look like you've been dragged through a dust bowl."

Olive remained stone-faced. Lillian fingered her stiff red tendrils. "Suppose so."

"Where'd you all come from?"

"From the Pend Oreille area," Lillian said. "We—"

"Just the two of ya?"

"Yes, ma'am." Lillian hoped she would let them rest before asking so many questions. "We—"

"You from that way?"

"Well, no. I—"

"What brings you here? Where you girls headed?"

"If we could—"

"Quit talking now. I bet you two are tired and hungry." The woman motioned for them to tie their horses to a hitching post. "Let's get you fed, bathed, then you can tell me all about it."

"Thank you, ma'am."

"Glad to have ya. And enough ma'amin' me. We're the Browns. I'm Jane and my husband's Thomas. He's around here somewhere. Fixin' a wagon wheel I believe. Probably in the barn." She waved them over. "Come on in. I'll heat water for a bath and fix you a bite to eat. You got names?"

Kids peaked over the fence and giggled. Lillian smiled at them. "I'm Do—er—Lillian Gardner and this is Olive Watts. Your kindness is appreciated, but we can wash at the creek. We'd be mighty obliged for a meal, though. Dried meat and, well, dried everything makes a person hungry for a hardy meal."

Jane chuckled. "I imagine so." She glanced behind them. "No family with you, huh?"

"We're alone. Headed home."

"Where 'bouts you from?"

Lillian motioned west. "Over them mountains."

"Oh, my. Well, I'll start cooking," Jane said. "Come on in when you're ready."

Lillian and Olive led their horses to a shallow creek on the west side of the barn—hidden by a thicket of buckbrush. After the horses got their fill of water, Lillian let them graze. She shed her hat, boots, shirtwaist, and skirt and ambled in. She cupped her hands and took several drinks before laying in the water and letting the current expand her underclothing. "Come on in!" She took a deep breath and submerged her head in the creek. She came up spitting and laughing. "This is delightful!"

228

Olive glanced around, took her boots off, and set her feet in the creek. She swirled her toes in the water, the hint of a smile on her face.

"You aren't going to get the dirt off if you don't come in."

"Where's Mister Brown?"

"I don't see him. It's all right. We are far enough away he won't see us even if he's outside. Besides, if he's fixing a wagon wheel, he's probably in the shade of the barn on a blistering day like this."

Olive glanced around before taking her dress off and wading in. She eased into knee-deep water and wet her face.

Lillian gave Olive a light splash, hoping she'd relax and have a little fun. But all she did was give a small smile. "Things will get better."

Olive shrugged. "Hope so."

"You can come home with me. I plan on asking my folks if you can stay. We raise cattle and chickens. Mama has the most wonderful garden. It's full of carrots, potatoes, squash, beans, peas…"

Olive grinned. "Sounds nice."

Two little girls skipped toward them, singing. One swung a basket. They stopped when they got to the creek. The older one said, "Mama thought you might need soap and towels."

Lillian waded to them. "How kind. Thank you."

The younger girl giggled. "I like bathin' in the creek, too. But only when it's hot outside."

"Come on in," Olive said.

Lillian jerked her head toward her companion, her brows lifted. How wonderful to have her talking again. She had no inkling Olive was fond of children.

The youngest girl dipped a toe in, but the older sister put out an arm and stopped her. "We have chores to finish. Anyway, Mama told us to give you privacy." The girls spun around and dashed away, giggles floating behind them.

Lillian and Olive washed, dressed, and trekked to the plank house. Freshly washed clothing hung from a line. Lillian studied the wooden structure. It was certainly different from her pa's log cabin. She wondered if they stayed warm in the winter with such thin walls. She stepped into the modest home.

"There you are!" Jane motioned for them to sit at a long table. Eight chairs lined the edges. The girls who joined them at the creek set scones and preserves on the table. Jane served fried chicken, mashed potatoes, green beans, dried peaches, and plum pudding.

"This is a feast fit for a king," Lillian said. "I can't thank you enough."

"It's no fuss at all. We've already eaten. All I had to do is warm it up." Jane wiped her hands on her apron and sat down with a cup of coffee. She nodded to her daughters. "You girls can dish yourselves some puddin'. A second helping never hurt anyone."

The females ate and got acquainted. When Lillian was on her last bite, a husky man burst into the house, carrying a young boy.

"He cut his leg open."

Jane jumped to her feet. "What happened, Thomas?"

Lillian slid the dishes over. "Lay him on the table." She turned to Olive. "Fetch the satchel and pouch tied to the saddle horn." Olive nodded and rushed out the door.

Lillian pressed a hand to the boy's shoulder. "I'm Doctor Gardner, can you tell me how this happened?"

The boy's body shook, and he gritted his teeth.

"Okay, we can worry about that later." Lillian turned to Jane. "Fetch me some clean rags and boil some water."

Jane nodded. "Thomas, stoke the fire." The man strode to the cookstove and added fuel.

Olive came in and set the satchel and pouch on the table. Jane shooed the girls out of the house and yelled for the others to remain outside. She came back with a few linen towels and a handful of flannel.

Lillian spread open the satchel and took out a needle and thread. She was surprised to see the contents were in good order. Although the supply of morphine was missing. She gave the boy a small dose of laudanum. "Olive, pour some chloroform on one of those flannel pieces and cover his mouth and nose."

"You want to knock him out?"

"We need to stop this shaking or I'll never get him stitched."

Olive did as instructed. The strong, thick smell of the anesthetic filled the room. When the boy finally went under, Lillian cleaned the wound which exposed muscle and bone. Her steady fingers looped small sutures along the seven-inch gash. Their eyes large, the boy's folks watched as Lillian sewed the inside layers first. She squinted, wishing she had better lighting.

When the laceration was closed, Lillian fetched rattlesnake plantain and alumroot from her pouch and salve from the satchel, made a poultice from the herbal concoction, and placed it on the sutures. She then wound the leg with strips of linen and tied a knot with the ends. When she nodded at Thomas Brown, he lifted his son and carried him to another room.

"I had no idea you were a doctor." Jane wrung her hands. "You're so young…"

"For the past several weeks I have studied under Doctor Mali Maddox." Lillian scrubbed her hands in a basin of hot water. Olive seemed upset and went outside.

"Where is this doctor now?"

Lillian took in a deep breath. "She passed away while we were with the River Paddlers near the Pend Oreille River."

"I see," Jane said. "I'm sorry for your loss. She trained you then?"

"She did. That's why I'm returning home." She cleaned the table, washed the needle, and sterilized both with vinegar. Then settled in a rocker near the hearth by Jane Brown and a cup of coffee and told her how she'd connected with the healer, their journey to the other side of the mountains, how she and the Watts siblings hooked up, and shared her future plans as a medicine woman.

"And what about Olive?" Jane fingered the rim of her tin cup. "What will happen to her?"

"I plan on taking her with me. I'm sure my ma will be happy to take her in."

"Oh…?"

Thomas Brown entered the kitchen. "He's asleep. I'm much obliged to you, Doctor." He glanced from his wife to Lillian. "Didn't know doctors came as young as you."

Jane laughed. "I'll tell ya all about her later, dear. Now, you go back to fixin' the wagon and let us girls chat, won't ya?"

He tipped his hat to Lillian and strode out the door.

Later that evening and after dinner, Thomas Brown approached Lillian as she sat on the porch, about ready to write in her journal. He was clean and his hair combed, the scent of lye soap on his skin.

"I wanna thank you for taking care of my boy."

"My pleasure. How is Landon?"

"He's awake and eating some of Jane's apple pie."

Lillian chuckled. "He's fortunate he didn't lose his leg."

The space pinched between Thomas's brows. "The missus said you're fixin' to head over the mountain to go home soon. You live near the Columbia?"

"Sure do. It's been a long time." *Too long.*

"There's a good Indian trail. I can draw you a map."

Lillian opened her journal to a blank page and handed the book and her fountain pen to him. "That would be most helpful."

He sketched the homestead, creek, valley, mountain range, and Columbia River. He put an "X" next to their house. "This is us."

Lillian smiled and nodded, figuring as much.

He drew a line from their house to the Columbia. "This is the Indian trail you'll need to follow." He tapped the end of the line that ran into the Columbia River with the end of the pen. "From here, I 'spect you'll know which direction you'll need to go."

Lillian studied the map. "I think once I get to here"—she tapped the end of the trail—"I'll have to head south for a bit."

"Mmm." Thomas nodded. "Your pa and Jack Dalley run cattle, don't they?"

Lillian raised her brows. "You know Jack and my pa?"

"Never met 'em but hear they have the best beef around."

Lillian chuckled.

"I reckon if you travel at a fast pace, it'll take ya a couple days." He sat back on the steps. "It'll be a hard journey at times, but I know if you've come this far, you'll have no troubles."

"I hope so. I'd like to enjoy the ride home."

"The missus shared your excursion with me." He whistled long and low. "You got anything to clean your six-shooters with?" He winked at her.

"No, sir, I don't."

"Get 'em to me and I'll fix ya up." His gaze landed on the valley. "You're welcome to stay as long as needed. Miss Olive too."

CHAPTER 38

August 24

Lillian leaned her back against a pole supporting the porch, her knees drawn up toward her chest. Gratitude filled her heart. So did a steady stream of anxiousness.

I know it was you, Lord, who sent us to the Browns. Tonight I am thankful for your guidance and protection. I feel safe here in this valley with Thomas and Jane Brown. Taking care of Landon has helped me make up my mind about being a doctor. I will not become a doctor like Mali but do desire to help others.

I rather like the idea of becoming a medicine woman—a nature healer of sorts.

To do that I must recover from this ordeal. I so hate my nightmares. Please take them away, Lord. Over and over I see his greasy face hovering over me, threatening me, a gun to my face. I hear the click of a misfire and his taunting laughs. I wake up soaked with sweat and feel as though I had not slept. Will the visions never end?

I am also troubled over Olive. Perhaps that is not the right word.

She pulled the pen away and took a deep breath, rubbed her neck.

I suppose I'm somewhat at odds with the Browns' offer.

Lillian leaned her head against the pole. A heaviness clenched her chest.

I am not sure what Olive will choose, to remain here with the Browns or come with me. I want her to come. But is that selfish? Should I allow her to choose what is best for her? Is she old enough or presently in the right mind? What would make her most happy?

Perhaps it is rejection I am feeling. Rejection stemmed from the surprise of their offer and the look on Olive's face when they asked. It is clear she is happy here. Perhaps it is fear of traveling alone after our attack.

I pray for guidance. Maybe I will stay on and make sure that is what is best for Olive and see that the Browns are sincere about their proposal. I have to know in my heart Olive is safe and will thrive in her new environment.

Maybe I am getting ahead of myself and after she ponders the offer, she will decide to come with me. I will give her the space to choose on her terms.

It is nice here. They seem like an amiable family. Trustworthy souls who truly care about others. I suppose it is fatigue that stirs my uneasiness.

For now, I will sleep. Things will surely look better in the morning when I am fresh. I must remember there is a time for everything under the sun.

CHAPTER 39

"You sure you want to stay here with the Browns?" Lillian asked Olive as she tapped her Stetson over her red braids. She brushed a stray curl out of her face and tucked it behind an ear.

Olive nodded. "Once I've had enough schooling, I can help. I've always been interested in teaching. Maybe I can help form a school. I'm sure in no time this will become a booming town and they'll need someone to teach the children. I'd sure like the job."

"They'd be lucky to have you."

Jane walked up to the girls and held out a pail to Lillian. "Here's a little something for your journey."

Lillian took the pail. "You have done so much for us these past few days."

"It has been a pleasure to have you." Jane grinned. "You fixed up our Landon. It's the least we can do."

Lillian hugged Jane. "You and your family are blessings to all who pass by."

"Sure you don't want to stay on as well? We need a good doctor around here."

Lillian hugged the pail. "It's time I get on home. I have some explaining to do to my folks."

"If you're sure then."

Lillian hugged Olive, said her farewells, and mounted Asa. "I hope to see you all again someday."

Olive handed her Chwim's lead. "You sure you want to leave the other two horses here?"

"I'm sure," Lillian said. "You'll need dependable mounts." She waved and reined Asa west.

The trail was easier to follow than she'd assumed. On her way up the mountain, she came across several Sinyekst men on their way back from trading with the Flatheads in Montana Territory. They often traded salmon for buffalo hides and dried meat. It pleased her to visit with them in the familiar Salish dialect.

When Asa began to slow down, she stopped at a pond to water and rest the horses. She fetched the pail Jane had sent with her and popped open the lid. Inside was a scone, bacon, apple, and a piece of peach pie. Olive had made the right choice to remain with the Browns—a truly hospitable family.

Lillian was about to bite into her scone when a man on a thick black horse appeared around a bend several yards before the pond. She squinted her eyes. Something seemed familiar about him, making her belly clench. The closer he got, she could see he didn't appear to be friendly. She rose and calmly strode to Asa and tried to lift the rifle from the scabbard, but something held it in place. Even though she gave it a good tug, it wouldn't budge.

"Don't move, girly." The man pointed a six-shooter at her. The metal glinted in the sun, causing Lillian to shade her eyes.

Girly. He was a spitting image of Seth, but Lillian was sure the outlaw was dead. She studied him, noticing the man before her had lighter hair than Seth. If he wasn't the

238

desperado, then who was he? "I'm not looking for trouble. I'm simply headed home."

"You ain't lookin' fer trouble, huh?" He sneered at her. "Too late, girly. You done killed my brother."

She cleared her throat, her knees wanting to buckle. All she wanted to do was go home. "And who was your brother?"

"Don't you go playin' no games with me." He spat a long stream of brown juice from his mouth.

"Like I said, I'm not looking for—"

"Trouble. So you say." He dismounted, landing tenderly on one leg. "Seth wasn't as smart as me. I won't fall asleep and let ya get away."

There was more than just the two of them. "I don't know anyone by the name of Seth, perhaps you are mistaken."

"There ain't no mistake. I saw him talkin' to you near the Pend Oreille River. I told him to leave you alone. But he didn't listen. He's always been drawn to pretty redheads. I knowed he followed you. It was you who killed him. I just don't know how one little girl as wispy as you could have killed two beefy men. Then I saw that fella you was with, was he your mister?"

"My what? No…!"

"Who was he, then?" The man took a few steps toward her.

Lillian backed up. She sure wasn't about to mention Olive if he hadn't seen her. "He was just a nice man who came to my rescue after your brother and his companion ambushed me."

"You shouldn't have teased him at the river."

"Tease him?" Heat rose up Lillian's neck. "I stitched his cut." *I should have left before he even got close to me.* She prayed the man would come to his senses and move on. Or the Lord would send a group of Indians to help her.

"I saw you carryin' on—" He limped a few steps toward her.

"I did no such thing!" Lillian pulled her knife from her boot and held it out. "Leave me alone, mister."

He gave her a lopsided grin. "Now you've gone and done it. I'll have to kill you for sure." He limped closer.

She jabbed the knife in the air.

He lunged at her, knocking her to the ground. "I'll show you—"

"Get off me!" Lillian bit his ear, shoved him off of her, and sprang to her feet. She spat in the dirt, leaving a red stain.

He howled, pressing a hand to his bleeding lobe, rolled over and got to his knees. "You are a feisty one."

Lillian flung her knife at him, the blade sticking in his shoulder. She took several steps backward. He hollered and dropped to his knees. After pulling the knife out, he leaped to his feet and started after her. Lillian gathered her skirt and bolted, not knowing the territory or where she'd end up.

With no weapons, she ran as fast as her legs would carry her. He hobbled behind her.

"Stop!" He shouted.

She scrambled up a hill and came to a ledge. As a shot rang out, she dropped to the ground. Air scraped her lungs with every rapid breath.

He came into view, clutching his bloody shirt. "I'm gonna kill you, girly."

She rolled behind a boulder, her mind scattered. *How can I get away from him? What can I use as a weapon?* The trees were too far away. The rocks not big enough. She was not David from the Bible and did not have a sling-shot. The man was not a giant. But if God allowed David to bring a rock to a sword fight and kill Goliath, he would protect her too. He had to. He promised. God had prepared David for years tending sheep. How had he prepared her? Her guns were with the horses. Her knife was who knows where…

"Come on out," he said. "I don't wanna kill you. I was mad. Blamed you for my brother's death."

She winced. "You're asking me to trust a man who threatened to kill me and then shot at me. You're crazy! Both you and your brother are plum out of your minds!" From around the rock, he staggered, holding a leg.

"I'm hurt. My leg's swollen and infected. Seth told me you're some kinda doctor."

"He was wrong." Why her? Surely, he could find someone to help him.

"He told me you have a big bag of medicine and I know you stitched him up."

Footsteps came closer. "Here. Take a look. I'm tellin' the truth."

Lillian held a hand over her mouth. Even the thought of being a healer now made her want to retch. She craned her head around the rock. Her knife lay on the ground. Light glinted off the blade. He saw it too, grabbed it before she could, and sliced his trousers, exposing a swollen thigh. She shook her head, tasting the bile rising up her throat. "Nothin' I can do. If I were you, I'd ride to Fort Colville and have the surgeon take a look."

"Nope. That won't work. I don't need my leg cut off."

"What do you expect me to do?" Lillian pursed her lips. "I don't have any medicine that will help you. Nor the skills."

He waved his pistol in the air. "It hurt too much to ride that far. Now, come on out and help me. That lady doctor must have taught you more than you're claiming to know."

Lillian recalled Doctor Maddox telling her about a procedure called bloodletting. It was mainly used with patients affected with consumption, dropsy, hydrocephalus, gout and other diseases of the body. Most doctors would allow the patient to bleed until they were almost faint. She could just let him bleed out until he was dead. "I may have something that will help."

He laughed. "I knew you'd listen to reason." He cocked his head. "Why don't you come out from behind the rock and explain it to me."

Lillian pushed to her feet, keeping the boulder between the two of them. "How do I know you won't kill me after I fix your leg?"

"I'm not a killer."

"Then what are you?"

His smile made her cringe. "I'm in the business of taking things from those who are a little more fortunate than me."

"You're a thief, is what you're saying."

"Now, that's not nice—"

"And neither is robbing innocent folks."

His face twisted. "Tell me how you're gonna fix my leg."

Lillian stiffened. "It's a procedure doctors have used for centuries."

"I'm listenin'."

"It's called bloodletting, have you heard of it?"

He tipped his head and blinked several times. "Don't think I have."

"Well, I'd have to make a small incision in your leg and drain the pus and blood—"

"You ain't gonna cut me none."

"Well, you can make the trip to Fort Colville if you want."

He shook his head. "Okay then. How much blood?"

"Not much," Lillian said. "Our bodies have a whole lot of blood in them. It won't take much. You won't feel a thing." She sucked in a slow breath, praying he'd fall for it.

He narrowed his eyes and stared at her for a long moment. "Fine. But if you try any shenanigans, I'll shoot ya dead."

"I understand." She smiled. "You don't mind if I give you something to relax, do you? I might take a little of it myself."

"What is it?"

"A mixture of lemon balm and chamomile."

"Sounds like some kinda girly remedy to me."

"I can show you." Lillian stopped herself from naming Doctor Maddox and him thinking she stole the satchel. "It's in my medical bag."

"You look too young to be a doctor."

"I studied under one for the past several weeks." She wished he'd believe her and quit testing her so she could hurry up and get back to Asa and her pistols.

He eyed her. "Like I said, you try to trick me, you're good as dead."

Chapter 40

Lillian handed him the herbal tea to settle his nerves and went to fetch the medical satchel. She was afraid if he didn't have something soon, his shaky hands would pull the trigger. She needed to get to her pistols. If only she had her knife.

A hefty dose of laudanum is what he needed. Lillian felt he would explode anytime and kill her. She wished she had sewn secret pockets into her skirt like Hannah had when she raced horses. The male racers had been so malicious, her sister used to tuck a small pocketknife into a hidden pocket at the skirt band. Lillian's boot simply wasn't secure enough.

"What's takin' you so long?" he said. "This tea water ain't doin' nothin'. I need somethin' stronger."

Stronger. That was it! "You have some whiskey on you?"

"As a matter of fact I do." His voice softened, making Lillian relax. "Check my saddlebags."

Lillian found a glass bottle and uncorked it. She wrinkled her nose at the pungent odor drifting from the container. Then smiled. *This will do.*

"Find it?"

"Sure did." She squatted, holding back a cackle, and mixed the liquids. His eyes were closed, his pain evident by his tense jaw, so she quickly reached for one of the pistols in her saddlebag—

"Get over here and fix my leg!" He waved his six-shooter at her.

Lillian jerked at the raw tone in his voice. "I have to clean my instruments, mister..." She raised a brow at him.

"My name's Spade, girly."

"That your given name?" She unrolled a leather case of assorted knives, chose a small sharp one, and wiped it off with a whiskey-drenched cloth. She tucked a longer one in the back of her skirt band.

He scowled at her. "That's what you'll call me." He shook his head and examined his leg.

She took his distraction to slip one pistol in her boot and the other in the satchel. All she needed to do was to keep his wandering eyes out of the bag. "All right then, Mister Spade it is."

"Just Spade," he said. "My leg's gettin' redder. You almost done?"

What a greenhorn. "I'm going as fast as I can." Lillian shook her head. "I can't cut into you with a dirty knife, now can I?" But she wanted to. "Your leg will only get infected again."

"Well then, hurry up."

She poured some laudanum tainted whiskey in a tin cup and took it to him. "Here, drink this."

Spade grabbed it from her and downed it. "Give me another."

Gladly. Inside, she smiled and poured him another. "Here's too good health!"

He gulped the drink and slammed the cup in the dirt. "I'm ready." He gave her several rapid nods and squeezed his eyes shut."

A grated snicker erupted from Lillian's mouth. "You scared of…?"

He opened one eye. "I ain't scared of nothin'. Now, do your blasted job, woman!" He closed the eye.

Woman. She snorted, feeling sorry for their mother, wondering if she was a sweet woman who bore wretched sons or if she was just as cantankerous. What was his real name? "Hold steady now." With a shaky hand, she washed the infected area and put the tip of the blade to his leg.

"Why ain't you cuttin'?"

She startled, a squeal coming from her lips.

"Thought you was a doctor."

"I am," Lillian said. "Your impatience isn't helping me."

"Take a swallow of the whiskey." He motioned for her to get him another drink. "I'll take one too. It'll calm both our nerves."

She shook her head. "I do not drink spirits or any other form of firewater."

"I bet you're the prayin' kind."

"That I am." Lillian grinned at the slight slur in his words. *It won't be long now.* Her belly fluttered as she examined his red-streaked leg. "How'd you get this gash, anyway?"

His eyes drooped. "Youuu…"—he took in a long breath and let it out—"almost done?"

Lillian held up the knife. "Yep." She sliced the blade through a thin layer of skin. Thick greenish-yellow pus oozed from the wound. Guess it didn't matter how he got the cut. It was best she didn't know the circumstances.

She poured him another drink. "Take this. It'll keep the pain away that much longer."

He downed the whiskey mix and plopped his head back on the ground, his eyes closed. When Lillian was sure Spade was out, she untied his neckerchief, poured a small amount of chloroform on it, and laid it over his nose and mouth. She had to be sure he'd stay asleep for a while. She scooted back, his leg laid open and draining, and placed some of the items back in the satchel. Sterilized others. Then kneeled on the ground and chewed her bottom lip, waiting for the chloroform to take full effect.

As much as she wanted to hurry and gather her belongings and gallop away, she couldn't just leave him. He was the cruel one. Him and Seth. She couldn't be like them. Wouldn't be as despicable as the brothers.

She wondered what her own brother was up to. How the cattle were faring. Home called to her. Mama would be deep in garden harvest, Pa thinking about weaning calves.

After several minutes, she stood and brushed off her skirt. "You're not worth it, but I have a job to finish." She cleaned his infection, packed the wound with rattlesnake plantain, and wound strips of flannel around his leg. She picked up the bottle of whiskey and stood over him. He lay still as a rock, his rotten hide stinking like a decaying badger. She leaned over and poured the remaining whiskey on his leg, tossed the bottle, and grunted. He moaned and clawed at his leg. She stiffened, ready to get more chloroform, then relaxed as he reclined and went back to sleep.

"May you and your brother rot in hell." Lillian gathered her supplies, his six-shooter and black horse, and Chwim and mounted Asa. After taking a moment to make sure she got everything, she kicked her bay into a trot and took off down the trail. Partway down the road, she reined Asa to a halt. She should have killed him. Now he would follow her. Find her. Kill her and her family. She turned the bay around.

Her mind told her to keep going. But her gut reminded her she was not like them. She was not a murderer. In the distance, a deer bounded from the brush and stopped on the trail. It gazed at her as if God himself was warning her. *Turn around. Go home.* A chill pricked the back of her neck. The deer darted across the trail and disappeared into the trees. But what if he did come after her? She was still having bad dreams. His attack would only make them worse. Killing him was the only way they'd stop.

She urged Asa back to the site. When they got there, the spot he had been laying in was empty. She swung her gelding around, searching. Where was he? She jumped off her bay and found his tracks. Three sets of large footprints imprinted the dirt. She followed them for a bit. They led east for a while before veering into the trees.

Lillian clenched her teeth, her body trembling. "I should have killed you!" she shouted. Her voice echoed off the rock bluffs. She gathered the two lead ropes, hopped in the saddle, and raced off, praying he would not come after her.

CHAPTER 41

The evenings are cool, but I am afraid to start a fire. I do not want to call attention to myself. I simply want to get home to the security of my family. I know Spade is out there. He is a mean, killing thief. I suspect a liar too. One I will put a bullet into if he shows his face again.

Taking his horse may not have been the smartest move on my part. Then again, I did the black a favor by saving him from the hands of an outlaw. A sure-footed mount. He's been ridden hard and is as gentle as a butterfly. I'll call him Midnight. I plan on keeping him for payment.

Spade does not deserve as fine an animal as—

Crunch, crunch. Lillian froze.

CHAPTER 42

Lillian's hand flew to the six-shooter by her side as she tipped an ear to the sounds. Something like clawing bark followed the crunches. She cocked her pistol and listened. Other noises skittered the forest floor. Was it him? Wild animals? She swallowed the lump in her throat, suppressing a scream.

Was he back? Would he attack her? She laid the journal and pen down as quietly as she could. How many of them were there? Her body trembled. Shallow breaths expanded her lungs.

"Who's out there?" She rolled onto her knees and pointed the weapon to the noises.

Her horses shifted, their hooves cracking dried leaves. She swung the pistol toward the shadows. A horse snorted. Would this go on all night? *Am I hearing things?* After a long moment of silence, she settled against the tree, wondering if she should saddle Asa and head out. She decided to stay put. Spade was in bad shape and she doubted he would have traveled so quickly as to catch up with her.

Throughout the night Lillian drifted in and out, waking to the slightest stir, finding it hard to go back to sleep. Wondering if he'd come back. If the sounds of the night didn't wake her, her dreams did. She saw him coming for her, heard his voice, felt his touch, and jerked awake each time he tried to choke her.

Waiting for daylight, she snacked on dried meat and vegetables Jane had given her. The nourishment would keep her strong. When the slightest hint of light struck, she saddled Asa and the other two horses and headed down the trail. Several times she nodded off, rocking in the saddle and trusting her horse to stay on the path. At one point, she stopped and tied Midnight to Chwim's saddle and looped Chwim's lead over the saddle horn. After walking a short while to wake up, she got back into the saddle and continued down the trail.

It felt like days until the Columbia River came into view, its power gushing downriver. There was a long way to go, but knowing she was close livened her spirits. A surge of energy rolled through her and for the first time, she felt safe.

By late afternoon sweat ran down Lillian's back and her skin felt sticky. She stopped at a pond and let the horses drink, and then tied them each to their own tree so they would not fight. A towering hill to the north was the perfect place to spot anyone following her. She checked the knots in the lead ropes and hiked the grassy knoll. Trees blocked much of the path, but for as far as she could tell, no one was behind her.

The hike down was quick and by the time she got to the bottom, fatigue had caught up with her. *I'll rest for just a moment.* She found a shady spot near the pond and laid down, her Stetson over her face, crossed her ankles, and took in a deep breath. "Almost there…"

The sun hung over the mountains to the west when Lillian woke up. She rubbed her eyes and pushed to her feet. The pond's surface reflected light green grass and blue skies. She went to the bank, cupped her hands, and scooped up water. Its cool, sweet taste slid down her throat, waking up her mind. She stood and stretched her back, her arms over her head.

She turned to the horses and gasped. "Chwim!" Where did he go? He had been carrying the medical satchel. She called his name, darting from place to place, climbed the hill, and searched. "Chwiiim!" She jogged back to the other two horses and studied horse tracks. "Where are you?" Had Spade caught up to her? Did he steal her horse? Her mind whirled.

There were only horse prints embedded in the dirt. Lillian sighed, relieved there was no sign of Spade. "I have to find Chwim." She untied Midnight and Asa, mounted her bay, and kicked him into a gallop. The big black pulled back, taking Lillian with him. She sailed through the air and landed on her back, air gushing from her lungs. She squeezed her eyes shut, her head spinning. "Asa…!"

When Lillian felt she could remain upright, she eased to her feet, her hands out to her sides. "My hat." Her father had given her the brown felt hat for a birthday a few years ago. She couldn't lose it. She whirled around, wobbled a few steps, and located the Stetson. Once it was snug on her head, she gathered the horses and tried again, slower this time. She followed the horse prints leading back to S che wee leh.

The tracks veered off the trail and led her through the trees into a meadow. Asa whinnied. At the edge of the clearing and hidden behind brush a dark form lifted its head. The creature opened its mouth and answered the bay. Chwim trotted into the field, his head and tail high in the air. He raced to Lillian and the other two horses. She

255

caught his lead and rubbed his head. "Are you a naughty little pony or did someone untie your rope, huh?"

Lillian rode the meadow and its edges until she was sure she hadn't been followed. When she felt no one was around, she headed west toward the Columbia. By the time they reached the river it was almost dark. She rode the horses into the river and let them drink. When they had their fill, she strung a rope between three Ponderosa Pines and tied each horse to a section of the rope. They grazed on what little feed there was underfoot. She went to each horse and rubbed them down with handfuls of grass. "There will be plenty to eat tomorrow when we get home." *Home.* It never sounded so good.

CHAPTER 43

August 30

Lillian took a chance and lit a lantern. But only long enough to write an entry in her journal.

I planned on making it home today. It would have happened if Chwim had not broken loose. It was my fault for falling asleep. But I am sure I tied the knot tight enough. I remember examining it before climbing the hill to make sure we were alone.

Spade is alive. My bones can feel his wickedness. Is he that crazy to follow us with his bum leg? Could he be quick enough to catch up? I reckon if he had another horse he could have. It would be just like him to kill someone and steal a good mount. That fella is a ruthless sidewinder. I pray the Lord strikes him dead. He would deserve it. I am sorry if my words offend you, God, but I cannot be anything but honest with my feelings.

Hopefully, Olive is adjusting well and her nightmares have ceased. It will take time and support from the Browns for her to heal properly. Certainly, her brother's death and Seth's attack opened mental scabs. I do hope someday we can see one another again. She is a gentle soul and I consider her a fine friend.

I should be home by the time Pa finishes the morning chores. Lord willing, he is home and not out horseback, checking the cattle.

It will be delightful to tell him about Thomas Brown knowing of him, Jack, and their stock.

My twisted insides warn me Mama will be angry. I deserve her displeasure. Hopefully, she will remember when she was orphaned and came out west and understands the need for a girl my age to take a journey and find herself. The regret I have is not telling them I was leaving.

I pray they forgive me and can see the woman I have become. My leaving reminds me of the prodigal son Jesus talks about in scripture. I reckon I am their reckless daughter. I pray they will welcome me home like the father in the Bible welcomed his son.

If not, I do not know what will happen. I recall when Mama threatened Hannah with moving her to Aunt Erma's ranch in Montana. Will they do the same with me? Is Aunt Erma still alive? Would they send me somewhere else?

Lillian's muscles tightened. In the distance, she heard leaves rustle and blew out the lantern. When no other sounds came, she put her journal and pen in her parfleche and bedded down. Restless, she got up, checked to make sure her pistols and rifle were loaded, and leaned against a tree, the rifle in her lap.

Stars flickered, shadows moved about, and Lillian's heart fluttered. She pulled a blanket up to her chin and settled in for the night. "I better not fall asleep this time." If only she could make a fire and brew coffee.

CHAPTER 44

Dawn had not quite broke when Lillian's eyelids fluttered open. Her heartbeat drummed in her chest at the thought of seeing her folks. Elation and apprehension wrestled inside of her as she pressed a forearm over her eyes and groaned.

She took time to pray and ask God for what to say before getting ready. How to say it. Rising to her knees, she fetched her journal. Her hands shook as she read through random pages. They had to welcome her back, didn't they? Just as they had for Hannah all those times. They were loving. Understanding. Forgiving.

Weren't they?

Her belly queasy, she nibbled on dried fruit and the last of a scone. After washing and continued prayer at the river, she saddled horses and dragged her heaviness into the saddle. Is it real? Was she almost home? She inhaled, making sure she was still alone, and urged Asa forward. Midnight and Chwim lagged behind.

Hours later, the cabin came into view. Lillian's body quivered as she watched for activity from the hill that dropped to the homestead. She considered going to the river to wash and be presentable before greeting her family. Who was she fooling? Dragging things out wouldn't make things easier.

Yet, she wasn't quite prepared to face them. Then a whinny came from the corral. Buttercup, her mother's Palomino mare, ran in circles, stopped, watched them. Lillian stiffened, praying her four-legged friend would settle and give her a little more time.

Asa answered, his voice a low rumble. Lillian leaned forward and pressed a hand to his neck. "Sshh, I'm not ready." She stroked his soft hair. His aroma calmed her.

Elizabeth stepped from the barn, shading her eyes with a hand. She strode to Buttercup and tried to calm her. The mare whickered, bobbing her head in Lillian's direction. Elizabeth turned, watched. She took a step forward. Her hand crept to her lips, causing Lillian's belly to flutter.

Elizabeth took a few more steps and hollered, "Phillip!"

Phillip appeared from inside the barn, walking stick in hand. "What is it?" He joined his wife.

"She's home!" Elizabeth lifted her skirts and ran toward Lillian, her hat sailing off her head, exposing long blonde braids.

Moisture filled Lillian's eyes. She urged Asa forward, his ears swiveling back and forth. When she was close to her mama, she jumped out of the saddle and ran into open arms. Mother and daughter collided into a joyous embrace.

"My darling is home!" Elizabeth squeezed her daughter, her voice thick.

"I missed you." Lillian clung to her mother, taking in her familiar smell and touch. *Thank you, Lord, for bringing me safely home.* She held her mother for a long moment. Heavy footsteps rushed toward them. She recognized her father's shuffle, one a hard step, the other lighter. "Can you ever forgive me for running away?"

Elizabeth pulled back. "Running away?" She wiped her eyes.

"Lilly Pad, you're home!" Tears streaking his face, Phillip dropped his walking stick and drew his daughter into his chest. "You're safe." He held onto her so tightly she struggled to pull in a breath. "I missed you more than you'll ever know."

Lillian patted his back. "I'm home." His embrace had never felt so comforting.

Phillip released her. "We look forward to hearing about your adventures." He retrieved his walking stick and grabbed Asa's reins. "He looks strong and healthy. I knew you would care for him." Asa lowered his head when Phillip stroked his neck.

Lillian tipped her head. "You are not angry with me?"

Phillip and Elizabeth exchanged glances. Elizabeth looped her arm in Lillian's. "Let's get you cleaned up. I'll cook a hearty meal. You're as thin as a whip. Sounds like we need to sort some things out. But first, let's eat."

"Where's Delbert?"

"Checking cows with Jack. They'll be back later."

Lillian was thankful she would have time to "sort things out" with just her folks. While they took care of the horses, Lillian bathed in the river. She dropped her dirty clothing in a wash bucket on the porch and went inside. She braided her wet curls as she padded across her cramped bedchamber.

On the bed lay a mound of nicely wrapped gifts of buckskin and cloth, adorned with bows of hemp rope and ribbon. She recognized a yellow ribbon—her mother's favorite. Moisture blurred her vision, and she felt her chin quiver.

She arranged the medical satchel, parfleche, and buckskin pouch on the floor and seated herself on the edge of her bed. Her body sank into the softness of her bedtick. She looked forward to a good night's sleep. The top gift was wrapped in buckskin, a dried wild rose on top. She lifted the cone-shaped package from its perch and untied the rope made from tule stalk fibers. She peeled back each flap until the gift was revealed. She sniffed, wiped her eyes. It had to have been from Spupaleena.

Nestled in the leather casing stood a cedar basket hat. Woven into the light-colored fibers were dark brown triangles resembling steps attached to Vs circling the hat. She reached into the basket and pulled out a pair of moccasins. Beaded on the top were frogs resting on a lily pad. She brushed off the bottom of her feet and slipped them into the buckskin footwear. After inhaling the cedar of the hat, she settled it on her head.

She opened the remaining gifts, all but one: a new bridle, she guessed from Delbert; floral fabric she could stitch a couple of new dresses with; embroidered handkerchiefs; a large pouch of various herbs; and a note to look in the corral. It looked like her father's scribbled handwriting.

Her heart sank. If only she had been patient, they would have celebrated her special day into womanhood. Lillian did not feel she deserved the gifts.

The large present loomed over the sparkly decorated room. She reached for it and after a moment retracted her hand.

"Go ahead. Open it," her mother said from the doorway. She stepped inside and joined her daughter on the bed, nodded.

Lillian untied the yellow ribbon and let the cloth enveloping the gift slide off. She gasped and pressed a hand to her mouth.

"I'll help you unfold it." Elizabeth stood and grasped a corner.

Lillian dabbed her eyes, stood, and stepped back, unfolding the quilt. Four log cabins of various colors were stitched in each corner. In the center was a yellow square made from a piece of ribbon—Elizabeth's treasured ribbon.

"I meant to give you this before you left."

"You knew?"

Elizabeth nodded. "Doctor Maddox had spoken with your father and me before she left."

"She never mentioned it."

"We had scheduled a birthday celebration for you by the river. That's where everyone went after the wedding. To set out candles and cake. We figured with the heavy wedding meal, it would be best to serve something lighter, concentrating on desserts." Elizabeth gave Lillian a soft smile. "Spupaleena and her family were preparing pitch torches for the party."

Lillian released a flood of tears. "I'm—"

Elizabeth put a finger to her daughter's lips. "Normally you were so patient and understanding. We took your gentle demeanor for granted. But we'll discuss this after we fill our bellies.

Lillian wiped her eyes with the shoulder of her shirtwaist and nodded.

Elizabeth tapped the middle of the quilt. "The yellow hearth in the center is the light that will always be on in our home. These cabins represent our family's homesteads—one for me and your pa, Hannah, Delbert, and you. No matter where we are in this world, we'll always be tied together with this yellow ribbon which represents our love for one another. Each of us has a piece now. It's what binds us together. No matter who you marry or where you plant roots of your own, this will remind you of where it all began—with those who love you."

Lillian sipped the last of her mint tea. Her nerves were not as raw as when she had first greeted her folks. After she told them about some of the patients she and the doctor had come across; events at Meyers Falls and Fort Colville; time with the River Paddlers; Doctor Maddox's death, and coming across the Watts siblings, she said, "I need to explain some things to you."

She wasn't ready to scare them with the bandits. Especially knowing one was still alive. Not yet, anyhow.

"I think we do as well," Elizabeth said, "but you can speak first."

Lillian wiped her mouth with a linen napkin. She fingered the cloth. "I—uh—I need to apologize for leaving the way I did." Sadness reflected in her father's eyes. She wet her dry lips and continued. "The wedding…" She stuffed her bubbling emotions back with a sigh. "I felt I needed to go with Doctor Maddox and find my own path in life. Discover who I am."

"And did you?" Elizabeth smiled at her daughter. "Did you discover who you are?"

"I think so." She fetched her journal and handed it to her mother. "It's all in there. I am so blessed you gave me a means to record my excursion. I think it shows who I really am."

"Oh, it was not from me…"

"Who was it from then?"

"Your sister and Leslie."

Lillian's mouth fell open. "But Delbert told me it was from you."

Phillip chuckled. "Your brother got many things wrong that day."

"He made me think I was sneaking off—"

"And you weren't?" Phillip raised a brow.

Lillian's cheeks heated. "I am not going to deny my ill behavior. Seems my pity, pride, and impatience caused me the most harm. I can only hope you can forgive me."

"I agree, Lilly Pad. Besides, it was you who lost out," Phillip said, his tone gentle.

"Mama told me about the party." Lillian wrung her hands under the table.

"You will always be forgiven," Phillip said. "I think you may have learned a valuable lesson by missing your own celebration, don't you?" He waited for Lillian to agree. "You will have to apologize to Spupaleena and her family.

"I will."

"And your brother and Jack when they get here."

"Yes, sir." She took a sip of her tepid tea, hoping it would wash down the guilt and shame. She pointed to the journal Elizabeth was thumbing through. "I suppose it's a bit of my legacy."

"Oh?" Elizabeth rested the book on her lap. "And what legacy do you wish to leave?"

"Something Doctor Maddox said." Lillian thought for a moment. "No matter where we go, we should always leave a legacy of hope."

"Sounds like she was a wise woman. God rest her weary soul." Elizabeth drummed her fingers on the open book.

Phillip cleared his throat. "Have you opened all your gifts?"

Lillian shrugged. "I think so."

"Did you see the note?"

She nodded.

"Well, I reckon it's time for you to head to the corral then."

Lillian shook her head. "I don't—"

"Get going." Phillip nodded to Elizabeth. "We'll join you shortly."

Lillian pushed from the table and went outside. She strode toward the south side of the barn, stopping to pet Buttercup. In an adjoining corral, Asa, Chwim, and Midnight chewed hay. Chwim snorted and went on chewing. Lillian made her way around the barn and to the corral. In it stood a black and white colt. It had to be one of Jack's. The closer she got, she realized how the horse resembled Spupaleena's racehorse Bear. Could it be one of his offspring?

Mid-step, a hand wrapped around her waist, pulled her tight, and another covered her mouth. She tried to scream and bite, but a strong grip prevented her from doing so. "Hey, girly, told you I'd find you," he whispered.

His hot breath brushed the back of Lillian's neck. The more she struggled, the tighter he squeezed, so she relaxed, hoping he'd remove his hand. He dragged her deeper into the trees before shoving her to the ground.

"Make a sound and you're dead!" He pointed his six-shooter at her chest.

"What do you want?"

"What do I want?" Spade spat on the ground near her feet. "My horse for starters. Then you can fetch me that medical bag you've been packing around." He motioned to his leg. "You lied to me. You're no healer."

"I never—"

"I said keep quiet!" He waved his gun at her.

"You steal that off some poor soul?"

"Shut your mouth," Spade said, "you messed up my leg."

"I did nothing of the sort." Lillian shifted her weight. "You were the one that got shot or stabbed, or whatever happened to you. I'm sure you deserved it. And I am a healer. A mighty fine one at that!"

Spade shook his head, a greasy smile on his face. "You've gotten mouthy since the last time we talked." He strode toward her.

A shot cracked the air and Spade dropped to the ground. Lillian screamed and threw her arms over her head, curled into a ball. Her ears rang, and her body shook. *Protect me, God!* Jack appeared out of the brush on a tall red and white horse. He jumped off his horse and sprinted to Lillian.

"Jack!" She reached for him, and he helped her to her feet. Lillian hugged him tightly, his strong arms around her. His grip had never felt so reassuring.

"Where'd you come from?"

"I went to check on the colt and saw the scuffed tracks by the corral. I followed them here. You okay?" He put her at arm's length and examined her face.

Lillian let go of him and brushed off her skirt and shirtsleeves. "I'm fine. Was about to drop him myself."

Jack looked around. "With what?"

Lillian smiled. "My charm."

Jack hugged her and laughed. "I see you're back…"

CHAPTER 45

It was late evening when Lillian found time to sneak down to the river and write in her journal. Gratitude filled her heart plum full.

Everyone has seemed to calm down. Spade showing up forced my hand and I finally spilled the beans about him and his brother. Lord, I do not know how to thank you for protecting my family from the wretched man. Thank you for sending Jack. Maybe now you have forgiven me. I hope so. I know you do not like murder, but in the book of Ecclesiastes, you say there is a time to kill. I suppose it is to protect us from harm. And that outlaw is nothing but pure evil. I am glad he is dead.

You have taught me much these last weeks. The worth of honesty, how to love unconditionally, who to trust and who to run from, and the value of friendship and patience and mercy. You have given me knowledge and courage I did not know I had, and you have shown me the journey I need to be on.

You have revealed my pride and its destruction. At the same time, you have shown me how blessed I truly am. Please, never let me take my family for granted again.

Thank you for teaching me gratitude and your unfailing love and protection. As stubborn as I have been, you stuck with me.

I am thankful for so much. Not simply the gifts, this journal, or the magnificent new horse, which I am truly grateful for, but for family. Love. And roots.

I am thankful most of all for giving me the legacy of hope.

Welsh Dictionary

Dyfedeg - Southwest Wales

Yes – le

Nice to meet you. – Braf i gwrdd a ti or chi. Ti is good friend. Chi acquaintance or older person.

Girl – merch

Hello – helo

How are you? – Shwd mae?

Good morning. – Bore da.

Mother – mami

Blessing – bendith; Blessings to you – Shwd i ti is a friend or family, Shwd i chi if not.

Beloved, dear – Annwylyd, annwyl

Swift, Nimble – Chwim

Doctor – Meddyg

Please – Os gwellwch yn dda

Father – dadi

Look out! – Cymer ofal!

Boy/Lad – bachgen

Thank you, with thanks – Diolch

Good night – Nos da.

Sorry – Ma flin da fi

Oh, my – O na wyt ti'n iawn

God be with you – bydded duw gyda chi/ or ti again if you know them well.

For heaven's sake – er mwyn y nefoedd.

Don't be daft or ridiculous – paid a bod yn hurt.

Did you enjoy *Lillian's Legacy*? I hope so!
Would you mind taking a minute to leave a review?
https://carmenpeone.com/books/lillians-legacy/
It doesn't have to be long. Just a sentence or two telling
what you liked about the story!

~ ~ ~

To receive two FREE gifts and get updates when new
Carmen Peone books release,
click here: https://carmenpeone.com

Acknowledgments

Thanks to Dr. Maria Trevino for making sure all of my medical scenes were sound; Katie Tolin, curator for Stevens County Historical Society Museum, who took me on an 1800s medicinal tour; Sue Richart, who is on the Board of Directors and Treasurer at the Stevens County Historical Society and with The Heritage Network, for sharing all of your area research, documents, maps, and photos; Roni McFadden who helped me know the birthing process from the angle of a mid-wife and to confirm herbal healing properties; Brandon Finley for traditional tribal herbal knowledge and their traditional uses and traditional foods of the Kalispels in the Pend Oreille River area; JR Bluff for traditional Kalispell cultural practices; and Dr. Shawn Brigman for his expertise with traditional Plateau canoes; Sylvia Evert for putting me in contact with your father in Wales; John Williams and Julie Stephens for your assistance with Welsh language and customs. Because of you, Doctor Mali Maddox is an authentic character. Thanks to my editor, Leo Brickner, for helping to polish this story; Corinne Brown and Milana Marsenich for your wonderful insights. You have made this story shine! It takes a village to raise a child and write a story. My deepest gratitude to you all.

Teisen Afal (Avallon 'Apple' Cake)

Ingredients
½ lb (250g) apples
6 oz (170g) sugar
5 oz (140g) butter
1 lemon rind/peel grated
2 eggs
8 oz (225g) flour
1 teaspoon bicarbonate of soda
1 teaspoon, ground ginger
1 teaspoon ground mixed spice
1 teaspoon ground cinnamon
4 oz (115g) currants
4 oz (115g) raisins
4 oz (115g) mixed chopped peel
2 oz (60g) chopped walnuts

Peel, core and chop the apples and stew them with 1 oz (30g) sugar and a little water. When they are soft strain and leave them to cool.

Cream the butter and sugar and the grated lemon rind until light and fluffy.

Beat in the eggs one by one.

Fold in the flour sifted with the bicarbonate of soda and spices.

Stir in the dried fruit and nuts.

Mix all of this together, then carefully stir in the stewed apples.

Turn into a greased 7 inch (18cm) tin.

Bake at 350F (180C) for 1 to 1 ½ hours (60 to 90 minutes) until a skewer inserted into the cake comes out clean.

Enjoy this traditional Welsh dessert!

ABOUT THE AUTHOR

CARMEN PEONE is an award-winning author who resides on the Colville Confederated Reservation with her tribal member husband. She worked with Tribal Elder, Marguerite Ensminger, for three years learning the Arrow Lakes—Sinyekst—Language and various cultural traditions and legends. With a degree in psychology, the thought of writing never entered her mind, until she married her husband and moved to the reservation after college. She came to love the people and their heritage and wanted to honor her family with fiction true to culture and language as taught by elder Ensminger.

A horse enthusiast herself, she trains for and competes in local Extreme Cowboy and Mountain Trail competitions with her horse, Cash. She is a certified NASP archery youth instructor and coach.

Carmen loves to hear from readers.
Connect with her online:

Blog: https://carmenpeone.com/
Facebook: https://www.facebook.com/CarmenEPeone/
Pinterest: https://www.pinterest.com/carmenpeone/
Twitter: https://twitter.com/carmenpeone
Instagram: https://www.instagram.com/jcpeone/

Other Books By Carmen Peone

<u>Contemporary</u>
Girl Warrior

<u>True to Heart Trilogy - Historical</u>
Change of Heart
Heart of Courage
Heart of Passion

<u>Gardner Sibling Trilogy - Historical</u>
Delbert's Weir
Hannah's Journey

For information on YA Book Curriculum See Carmen
Peone's Website:
<u>https://carmenpeone.com/books/curriculum-young-adult-workbook-series/</u>

Made in the USA
San Bernardino, CA
28 July 2020

75672424R00173